IN
OVER
THEIR
HEADS

Also by Margaret Peterson Haddix

CHILDREN OF EXILE
Children of Exile
Children of Refuge
Children of Jubilee

UNDER THEIR SKIN
Under Their Skin
In Over Their Heads

THE MISSING
Found
Sent
Sabotaged
Torn
Caught
Risked
Revealed
Redeemed

THE SHADOW CHILDREN
Among the Hidden
Among the Impostors
Among the Betrayed
Among the Barons
Among the Brave
Among the Enemy
Among the Free

THE PALACE CHRONICLES
Just Ella
Palace of Mirrors
Palace of Lies

The Summer of Broken Things
The Girl with 500 Middle Names
Because of Anya
Say What?
Dexter the Tough
Running Out of Time
Full Ride
Game Changer
The Always War
Claim to Fame
Uprising
Double Identity
The House on the Gulf
Escape from Memory
Takeoffs and Landings
Turnabout
Leaving Fishers
Don't You Dare Read This,
Mrs. Dunphrey

MARGARET PETERSON
HADDIX

IN
OVER
THEIR
HEADS

UNDER THEIR SKIN BOOK 2

Simon & Schuster Books for Young Readers

NEW YORK LONDON TORONTO SYDNEY NEW DELHI

SIMON & SCHUSTER BOOKS FOR YOUNG READERS

An imprint of Simon & Schuster Children's Publishing Division

1230 Avenue of the Americas, New York, New York 10020

This book is a work of fiction. Any references to historical events, real people, or real places are used fictitiously. Other names, characters, places, and events are products of the author's imagination, and any resemblance to actual events or places or persons, living or dead, is entirely coincidental.

Text copyright © 2017 by Margaret Peterson Haddix

Cover illustrations copyright © 2017 by Shane Rebenschied

All rights reserved, including the right of reproduction in whole or in part in any form.

SIMON & SCHUSTER BOOKS FOR YOUNG READERS

is a trademark of Simon & Schuster, Inc.

For information about special discounts for bulk purchases, please contact Simon & Schuster Special Sales at 1-866-506-1949 or business@simonandschuster.com.

The Simon & Schuster Speakers Bureau can bring authors to your live event.

For more information or to book an event, contact the Simon & Schuster Speakers Bureau at 1-866-248-3049 or visit our website at www.simonspeakers.com.

Also available in a Simon & Schuster Books for Young Readers hardcover edition

Cover design by Krista Vossen

Interior design by Hilary Zarycky

The text for this book was set in New Caledonia.

Manufactured in the United States of America

0318 OFF

First Simon & Schuster Books for Young Readers paperback edition April 2018

2 4 6 8 10 9 7 5 3 1

The Library of Congress has cataloged the hardcover edition as follows:

Names: Haddix, Margaret Peterson, author.

Title: In over their heads / Margaret Peterson Haddix.

Description: First edition. | New York : Simon & Schuster Books for Young Readers, [2017] | Sequel to: Under their skin | Summary: Twelve-year-old twins Nick and Eryn and their robot stepsiblings, Jackson and Ava, try to save humanity from killer robots.

Identifiers: LCCN 2015039563| ISBN 9781481417617 (hardcover) | ISBN 9781481417631 (eBook)

Subjects: | CYAC: Science fiction. | Robots—Fiction. | Human beings—Fiction. | Extinction (Biology)—Fiction. | Secrets—Fiction. | Twins—Fiction. | Brothers and sisters—Fiction.

Classification: LCC PZ7.H1164 Ik 2017 | DDC [Fic]—dc23

LC record available at https://lccn.loc.gov/2015039563

ISBN 9781481417624 (pbk)

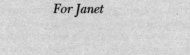
For Janet

IN
OVER
THEIR
HEADS

PROLOGUE

Lida Mae

The warning alarm woke Lida Mae from the deepest of sleep. Its wail was like a cross between an air-raid siren and a foghorn, and Lida Mae knew instantly what it meant, even though she'd never heard it before. Lida Mae was twelve; the alarm had never before sounded in her lifetime. If her parents and grandparents were to be believed, it hadn't gone off in centuries, not since it was first installed.

Lida Mae sprang from the pallet where she'd been sleeping and rushed to the nearest security screen embedded in rock. Her family had always been people of the woods, people who chose to live in a cave. She knew as well as anyone that this could be a false alarm caused by a squirrel or a raccoon or a bat chewing a wire. The death squawk of an inferior creature.

But the security footage flowing across the screen showed two children, a boy and a girl, standing before a broken desk in a sterile room. While Lida Mae watched, the children lifted papers from inside the desk, sank to the floor, and began to read. The children both had dark hair and dark eyes, which grew more and more solemn the longer they read. They both wore jeans and flannel shirts. The girl wore a hooded sweatshirt, too, but Lida Mae could still tell that both kids hunched their shoulders the exact same way. Perhaps these kids were twins. Perhaps they were about Lida Mae's age. Perhaps, in another lifetime, under different circumstances, she might have met them on a playground and they would have become fast friends.

She could sense her family crowded behind her, watching too, over her shoulder. But they stayed a respectful distance away. She had been first up, first to respond. This was her responsibility.

"Have you . . . ?" her mother murmured.

"Not yet," Lida Mae said, although she couldn't have explained what she was waiting for. A sign from the children, maybe, some indication whether they would be enemies or friends, just by their very nature.

She drew in a breath, preparing to speak a command, when the children on the screen suddenly looked up, startled. Lida knew they were only staring at the door of their sterile room, but it felt like they were staring at her; it felt like the surprise and fear mingled in their expressions were her fault. They scrambled to tuck the papers they'd been reading into their clothes, out of sight. Either they didn't know who was coming for them, or they did, and they were terrified.

The door of their room opened, letting in four adults and two more children. The room was full now, crowded with hugs and scoldings Lida Mae could sense without quite hearing.

Family, she thought. *That's how families behave.*

She managed to make out names from the faulty audio of the security system. The first two children who'd arrived in the room with the broken desk were Nick and Eryn. The other two were Ava and Jackson.

"Child . . . ," her mother prompted from behind her.

"I know," Lida Mae said. She squared her shoulder, lifted her chin, and addressed the security screen. "Analyze."

It felt like the security screen was thinking, though Lida Mae understood that this was a fanciful view of things. The security camera was linked to only the most primitive of computers. It was capable of only the most rudimentary calculations; it could no more think than a chicken with clipped wings could fly.

"The first two children—human," a voice devoid of emotion sounded from the screen. "The other two—robots. All the adults—robots."

Lida Mae's family gasped behind her.

"That's . . . complicated," her mother whispered.

"I can handle it," Lida Mae said, standing up straighter, taller. "I'll take care of everything."

ONE

Ava

Ava tried to catch her twin brother as he fell.

She and Jackson had been walking with the rest of their family through a dark cave, away from the odd room where they—and their stepsiblings—had learned a dangerous secret. Ava could tell Jackson was off-kilter. Thanks to her illegally enhanced vision, she could see him weaving and squinting and grimacing even though there wasn't enough light for anyone else to notice. His sandy-brown hair flopped around like a distress flag.

"Jackson, be careful!" she hissed. "Just stop thinking about—"

He was already stumbling, already dropping to his knees, already plunging face-first toward the rocky ground.

Ava grabbed for him, managing to catch his elbow with one hand and his armpit with the other. A year ago, when she and Jackson were both roughly the same size, that would have been enough for her to hold him up. But Dad had studied human growth charts, and he'd designated age twelve as the time when his son should grow five inches taller than his daughter and put on twenty pounds of muscle mass.

Well, not exactly muscle, Ava corrected herself, even as she cried, "Mom! Help! Jackson is . . ."

Mom reached for Jackson from the other side, but it was too late, and they were all too unbalanced. Gravity took over. Mom and Ava slammed to the ground along with Jackson.

"Oh no! Ava, Jackson, are you okay?" Mom cried, her first concern the children's well-being, as always. It was maddening. "Someone, please, a flashlight . . ."

Immediately Ava, Mom, and Jackson were caught in a ring of light. Even Ava's superior vision was temporarily blinded by the glow, so she couldn't see who was training a flashlight on Jackson's embarrassing moment and who was just standing there gawking. But she could count shoes, and everyone had circled around the piled-up Lightners: Ava's stepsiblings, Eryn and Nick Stone, who were also twelve-year-old twins; Dad and his new wife, Denise, who was Eryn and Nick's mother; and Denise's ex-husband, Donald, who was the other kids' father.

Oh, yeah, we're just like a traveling circus troupe, Ava thought. *Come one, come all, to see the happy blended family! Stepparents, stepchildren, stepsiblings—everyone getting along!*

Ava truly hoped they could all get along. But that seemed impossible now, given the papers she'd seen Nick tuck under his flannel shirt when the rest of the family found him and Eryn in the cave's secret room.

"Zzzt, zzzt," Jackson said, quivering as if he was totally shorting out. It was a sound that made Ava feel queasy and dizzy and in danger of falling apart herself.

Don't listen, she told herself. *Tune it out. Pretend . . .*

Pretend she was normal. Pretend she was just an ordinary kid. Pretend she was human. Like Eryn and Nick.

"Is he . . . *broken* again?" Eryn asked, taking a step back.

Ava wished her vision weren't quite so good. She wished she couldn't see the disgust on Eryn's pretty, normal, *human* face.

"Can anyone fix him, way out here in the middle of nowhere? In a cave?" Nick asked. Ava tried to give him the benefit of the doubt: Maybe he actually cared. Maybe he was trying to help. Not just pointing out how weird and troublesome Jackson was. "Don't you need *electricity* or something?"

He made electricity sound bizarre and risky and outlandish.

If Jackson were upright and alert right now, he'd probably have a snappy comeback, maybe, *Oh, and you don't ever use electricity yourself?* But Dad had programmed Ava to be more sweet and kind than that. She couldn't do snappy comebacks without worrying that she'd hurt someone's feelings.

Or maybe she'd learned that from Mom.

"Don't worry," Mom said, shoving back her curly red hair, which was just a little longer and thicker and more flamboyant than Ava's. Mom smiled reassuringly up at Nick and Eryn. "Any of us adults can help Jackson. We just have to, uh . . ."

She pointed to her stomach and pantomimed opening her coat and shirt.

Ava scrambled up and away from Mom and Jackson, almost crashing into Eryn, just as Eryn shoved her flashlight into her dad's hands and turned her head and took a step back.

Eryn was trying to get away from Mom and Jackson too.

"Ugh, Mom, do you have to talk about it?" Ava asked. "And *please* don't do that in public! Not when you have to expose your . . ." She stopped herself from saying "wires." She knew Nick and Eryn already knew that Mom—and all the other adults *and* Ava and Jackson—had wires and circuitry hidden inside their bodies, in all the places where Nick and Eryn had normal human organs and blood vessels and bones. But, knowing Mom, she'd probably try to turn the rebooting of Jackson into a science lesson for the kids.

So humiliating.

"Ava, we're hardly in 'public,'" Dad scolded. "We're in a cave that doesn't show up on any map, surrounded by a fifty-two-thousand-acre nature preserve that nobody but our family has visited in more than a decade. We're *safe*."

"Except for the possibility of sinkholes and rock-slides," Ava muttered, which made Nick almost grin at her.

Almost.

Ava envied Eryn her normal-human-girl vibe—like the way she could roll her eyes without the slightest mechanical hesitation. But Nick seemed more likable. More sympathetic.

"Ava, you're reaching an age where it's understandable for you to have concerns about the changes in your own body," Ava's stepmother, Denise, said, in her usual middle-school-psychologist soothing voice. "It's perfectly natural for preteens like you to transfer some of that anxiety into embarrassment over your parents' bodily natures. But there's nothing to be ashamed of."

Ava did not envy Nick and Eryn, having their every move psychoanalyzed and explained to them their entire lives. Since Dad and Denise had gotten married, six months ago, Ava had learned to avoid Denise as much as possible.

"Why don't the three kids go sit over there while Jackson reboots?" Denise's ex-husband, Donald, suggested, pointing toward a vaguely couch-shaped rock off to the side. "That'll give Brenda more space to work."

Ava liked how he made it sound like it would be a kindness—not cowardice—for the kids to walk away. She didn't know Donald well, but she would have preferred him as a new stepparent over Denise.

Maybe he and Mom . . . ? she thought.

She made the mistake of glancing from Donald to Mom again. Mom was bent over Jackson and had started unzipping her coat. Ava's head went woozy.

It's not embarrassment over my parents' "bodily natures," Ava thought. *It's that Mom's body isn't real. It isn't human. Just like my body isn't human. And Jackson's body isn't . . .*

"Go on," Donald said, giving Ava a gentle nudge. "You'll be okay."

Eryn and Nick hesitated, but Donald gave them a push too, and they followed Ava toward the rock. Still, none of them sat down. Eryn and Nick slid their hands into their jeans pockets and hunched their shoulders. Probably they were just trying to stay warm, since they'd both left their coats back at the campsite, outside the cave. But the identical motion made them seem sneaky, maybe even conspiratorial. Ava saw them dart glances at each other.

They're both human, and I'm not, Ava thought. *I'm outnumbered. Defenseless. What if . . . what if they decide to follow the instructions on the papers hidden under Nick's shirt?*

For the first time since the odd room, she let herself think about the evil words she'd seen written on one of the papers—evil words about how humans needed to destroy robots.

Evil words essentially telling Eryn and Nick that

they needed to kill Ava, Jackson, Mom, Dad, Denise, Donald—and everybody else who wasn't human.

Maybe . . . maybe that isn't really what it said, she told herself, fighting dizziness and queasiness and the urge to tumble senselessly to the ground, just like Jackson. *I saw those words for only a moment before Nick hid the papers. I don't think any of the grown-ups even saw that he had papers. Maybe . . . maybe I was just imagining things. Maybe my vision isn't as good as I thought. Maybe I misread everything. Maybe . . .*

It was too hard to fight her own brain. She knew what she'd seen. Her vision swam; her mind sizzled. Her hearing zoomed in and out. In a second she was going to be flat on the ground, making *zzzt, zzzt* sounds herself.

"Did you just hear something?" Nick asked, cocking his head. "Like maybe . . . footsteps?"

Ava seized on this question as if he'd thrown her a lifeline. She tilted her head too, forcing herself to listen intently. For a moment she couldn't hear anything over the mechanical buzzing that had started in her ears, another sign that her system was going down. But she and Jackson had upgraded their hearing at the same time that they'd improved their vision, so she told herself that she owed it to her entire family to listen harder, to be their first line of defense.

She owed it especially to Jackson, who would really be in danger if any outsider saw him with all his innards exposed.

There, she thought, peering at a point off in the darkness. *That's where the sound's coming from. The footsteps.*

The noise seemed about as far away as if she were standing in the goal of a soccer field and the goalie at the other end was tiptoeing around. She took two steps toward that distant point, then changed her mind. No matter who—or what—she and Nick had heard, she couldn't let anyone else find out how strong her vision was. She retreated all the way back to the three adults clustered around Jackson and Mom, and grabbed her father's flashlight.

"Eryn and Nick and I need this for a minute," she muttered.

In a flash she was back by Eryn and Nick's side. She wasn't going to faint. Not with this distraction. Not when she needed to protect her family. She linked her arms through the other two kids' elbows.

"Let's go see what it is," she whispered.

"It's probably just some kind of animal," Nick said, his voice full of bravado. "Won't it just run away when we get close?"

Ava could tell that he wished whatever it was would just run away. He didn't need anything else to worry about tonight.

"It better not be a skunk," Eryn muttered.

Ava took four more steps toward the spot she'd pinpointed as the source of the footsteps. The footsteps hadn't sounded again since she'd grabbed the flashlight. Which meant whatever it was had frozen in place, rather than fleeing.

Because it doesn't know that in another step or two, now that I'm listening closely, I'm going to be able to hear it breathe, she thought. *Unless it's smart enough to hold its breath.*

Or maybe it was something that didn't have to breathe?

Ava and the other two kids took two more steps forward. Then a third. Ava narrowed her eyes.

Oh no. Oh no. Eryn is going to wish it was just a skunk. . . .

But she didn't say anything to the other two kids.

The three of them kept walking forward, the flashlight in Ava's hand casting its glow closer and closer to the distant point where they'd heard footsteps.

Oh, good grief, Ava thought. *How blind are Eryn and Nick? Do they both need glasses?*

Finally, a dozen steps later, Nick gasped.

"Is that . . . is that a *girl*?" he asked.

TWO

Eryn

Or a ghost? Eryn thought, because it was easier to start believing in ghosts than to accept that anyone else had found the secret cave that only Eryn's family was supposed to know about.

What if somebody else had also found the secret room and seen the secret papers Nick had swiped and stuffed under his shirt? What if somebody else decided to follow their awful instructions?

Eryn had been raised by robots. She didn't believe in ghosts.

She remembered the terrifying thought she'd had in the secret room, about how there might be killer robots hidden in the back of this enormous, possibly endless cave—killer robots left over from a time when robots had destroyed humanity, and the last humans of that era had had to resort to a risky, desperate plan involving frozen embryos and kind, caretaker robots to revive the species.

But now the papers under Nick's shirt said that even the caretaker robots were dangerous and had to be destroyed. Even the robots like Eryn's parents. And Ava and Jackson. And . . . this girl?

Though her heart thumped frantically and she *knew* she wasn't brave enough to take another shock, Eryn peered closely at the face caught in the beam of Ava's flashlight. It was hard to tell in such dim light, but the girl's eyes didn't seem to have the flat, fake sheen Eryn had learned to look for in robotic eyes.

"Oh, um . . . hello," the girl said, turning her head side to side to grin at all three of them. The movement was smooth, without any of the slight mechanical jerkiness Eryn associated with robots. "I'm Lida Mae Spencer. Who are all of you'uns? Where did you come from?"

The girl's voice had an old-fashioned twang that made Eryn think of hoedowns and barn raisings and quilting bees. The girl sounded and looked and moved like a real human being—not a ghost, not a robot, killer or otherwise. But it felt like something else just as impossible was true: that this girl, Lida Mae, had stepped out of the pages of Eryn's history textbook.

Beside Eryn, Ava lowered the flashlight, probably to be kind and direct the brightest part of the beam away from Lida Mae's eyes. Now Eryn could see that Lida Mae had long braids hanging down on either side of her thin face. She wore a thick gray wool sweater—possibly handmade—and odd, bunched-up pants that might have been cut down from a pair that had originally belonged to an older brother or father. Her boots were dead ringers for the kind kids wore in *Little House on the Prairie*.

Maybe Eryn was slow in absorbing all of this. Nick answered before she or Ava could get a word out.

"Uhhh . . . hi. I'm Nick, and that's my sister, Eryn," he said, pointing. "And my stepsister, Ava. And we're here because, uh . . ."

Wait—was he going to try to explain? Would he be stupid enough to tell the truth?

"Our family's on a camping trip," Eryn said quickly. "That's all."

"We didn't know anybody else knew about this cave," Ava said, and Eryn admired the way her stepsister could sound so calm and easygoing. She might as well be reciting math facts.

Ava's a robot, Eryn reminded herself. *What do you expect?*

What if Lida Mae could also tell Ava was a robot? What if she was some . . . historical reenactor/undercover agent, part of a troupe that traveled around secretly looking for robot kids who broke all the rules? Robot children like Ava and Jackson, who were completely illegal? And rule-breaking robot adults like Eryn's parents and Michael and Brenda, who'd created them?

For once, Eryn could understand why her mother always said Eryn had too much imagination for her own good. Why would anyone need historic reenactors—or any kind of specialist—to search for illegal robot kids like Ava and Jackson? The way Jackson kept spazzing out and breaking down, anyone who looked at him could tell he wasn't human. Even if his eyes didn't give him away, his behavior did. That was one of the reasons his parents—and Nick and Eryn's—had wanted to come out to the nature preserve to hide.

Eryn glanced back to make sure the grown-ups and Jackson were far enough away that Lida Mae wouldn't be able to tell what they were doing. Eryn could barely see the glow of their flashlights.

Are Nick, Ava, and I too far away from the adults? Eryn wondered. *Are we in any danger from this girl?*

Lida Mae threw back her head and laughed—a rich, throaty sound.

"Goodness," she said. "My family's been living in or

near Mammoth Cave for as far back as anyone remembers. Grandpap says one of our ancestors came over on the *Mayflower* and right away hightailed it to Kentucky to marry himself the daughter of a Shawnee chief. She was, like, Native American royalty. And that's who the whole Spencer family descended from. Of course we know about this cave!"

Eryn reached behind Ava's back to poke Nick in the side. She hoped he understood that she meant, *Are you listening to this? Listening closely?*

She wished she could just ask him out loud, *Could it be? Could this girl's family have survived even when all the other humans went extinct? Because they were hiding in this cave out in the middle of nowhere? Could they maybe not even know anything about robots?*

Nick poked her back, which Eryn took to mean, *Oh, yeah. And I've got questions, too. . . .*

Eryn could think of a lot more to ask.

But if Lida Mae's family has been hiding out in this area for generations, wouldn't they have seen the desperate scientists hiding frozen embryos for the future, for after the killer robots were gone? Wouldn't they have seen the robotic trucks coming back for the embryos right before we were born? Wouldn't they have seen the secret room?

Eryn hoped Nick had figured out some answers, not just more questions. She hoped he understood something she'd missed.

With all their poking each other back and forth, Eryn and Nick weren't coming up with anything to say to this strange girl, Lida Mae. Fortunately, Ava took control.

"But surely your family leaves sometimes," Ava murmured. "To go to the grocery or the mall or . . . how far away is the nearest town?"

Lida Mae laughed again. Even totally freaked out and worried, Eryn liked the other girl's laugh. It was the kind that made Eryn want to giggle too.

"I don't know, because I've never been to town," Lida Mae said, with a careless shrug that made her sweater slip off her shoulder, revealing the thin, worn strap of a cotton undershirt. "Even my mammy and pap haven't been in years. It's miles and miles and miles away, I guess. We've got our own sheep for wool, and we grow our own food, and we've got the bees for honey—what would we need from any town?"

"You're saying your family is totally self-sufficient?" Ava asked.

Lida Mae hitched her sweater back up and toyed with one of her braids.

"Can't say I've ever heard that term, 'self-sufficient,' before," she admitted. "But I reckon I can kind of puzzle out the meaning. It's true my family doesn't have much use for the outside world. We've got everything we need, on our own."

"So you're able to survive out in the wilderness without help from anyone?" Ava persisted.

There was something brittle in her voice now. Eryn wondered if Jackson had sounded like that before he collapsed. Maybe being robots didn't protect the two kids from getting emotional and anxious. Maybe collapsing was just how they dealt with it.

Eryn eased her arm around Ava, in case she'd need to hold her stepsister up. What if Ava collapsed and Lida Mae insisted on bringing out her whole backwoods family to help? What if they saw the same tangled wires and circuit boards inside Ava's body that had so horrified Nick and Eryn? What would they do then?

At least Nick and I already knew there was such a thing as robots, Eryn thought. *At least we were used to working on computers and . . . and . . .*

And Eryn wasn't sure she and Nick had recovered yet from the shock of finding out that Ava and Jackson were robots. Or of finding out that *everyone* in the world who was thirteen or over was a robot too.

But maybe that's not true, after all, if Lida Mae's family has been here for generations, Eryn thought. *Because if Lida Mae's parents and grandparents were robots, they'd be linked to the network with all the other robot adults. And my parents and Michael and Brenda would have known that they were here. They would have been able to find out everything the adults in Lida Mae's family knew about Mammoth Cave, by going through the robot network. . . .*

"So, hey, that's really cool about your family," Nick said, his voice oozing fake enthusiasm. Eryn hoped she was the only one who could tell how fake it was, just because she and Nick were twins. "That's pretty incredible that you don't need stores. We'd love to see your, uh, farm. Could you show us how it all works?"

Stop! Eryn wanted to scream at Nick. *What if this girl says,* Sure, come on, *and then we have to explain that we can't go because Jackson broke down and Ava's about to? Aren't you paying attention? Aren't you thinking?*

But Lida Mae didn't say, *Sure, come on.* She stood there frozen for a moment, caught in the beam of Ava's flashlight like some prehistoric creature trapped in amber.

And then she whirled around and ran away, deeper and deeper into the dark cave.

THREE

Nick

"You're sure this girl was real?" Mom asked. "Not a hallucination, not a figment of your imagination?"

"We all three saw her, Mom," Nick argued. "How could all three of us imagine the same thing?"

After Lida Mae ran away, Ava had turned around and dashed back toward the adults and Jackson. Without a flashlight of their own, Nick and Eryn had had little choice but to follow Ava. Now Nick wished he'd grabbed the flashlight from Ava and chased after Lida Mae instead.

But what if she'd led me somewhere dangerous? Nick wondered. *What if the papers under my shirt had fallen out while I was running, and somebody saw them?*

It was awful to see holes even in plans that had already been stymied. It made him feel like there weren't good choices anywhere.

How could there be, when he was carrying instructions

that said his life, his sister's life—no, the very survival of humanity—depended on him and Eryn becoming murderers?

Is it still murder if the only people you kill are robots? he wondered.

His head throbbed. His heart squeezed. He went back to listening to the grown-ups.

"You expect us to believe that some girl was wandering around this cave that absolutely no one knows about, which is covered by KEEP OUT signs, and it's the middle of the night, and it's dark . . . and she's not even carrying a flashlight?" Nick's stepdad, Michael, asked. "Or, I don't know—a flaming torch? I didn't see any light over there but yours. Really, kids, if this is just some prank or tall tale you're trying to spin, stop right now. We've got enough real problems to worry about."

Nick hadn't even thought about the fact that Lida Mae hadn't had a flashlight. And he'd kind of forgotten about the KEEP OUT signs on the outside of the cave.

"She didn't have a flashlight or a torch," Ava said softly. She looked down, as if trying to hide the anguished frown that had crept over her face. Then she looked back up, squinting slightly, which was probably the sweet, innocent Ava version of a defiant expression. "But Lida

Mae *did* have a light. A little one. She was carrying one of those old-fashioned jam or jelly jars, and it kind of glowed, like it had lightning bugs inside."

"Really?" Eryn said. "I didn't see that."

Nick hadn't either.

"The girl was holding it behind her back while she was talking to us," Ava said. "And then in front of her while she ran. I only saw it in the split second as she turned."

"Kiddos, it's *February*," Dad said. "There aren't lightning bugs around in Kentucky in February."

"Then it was some other kind of bioluminescent creature," Ava said, with more stubbornness than Nick would have expected of her. "Some bioluminescent *cave* creature. They exist. Mom made us read about them in science."

Nick saw the adults exchange glances. Sometimes Eryn acted like he and she could read each other's minds, just because they were twins. But the adults, as robots, actually could. It was like they were connected over a special robot Internet.

Or . . . can they still link together down in this cave, out in this nature preserve, when they're away from the net-work of all the other robots in the world? Nick wondered.

He didn't think so. He was pretty sure that here in this cave, his parents and Michael and Brenda were as cut off as a cell phone out of range of a cell tower. He'd never liked the thought of his parents being practically all-knowing. But now it scared him that they weren't. That they were just as blind and lost as he was.

"Okay, there you go, Jackson," Brenda said from the ground, where she was still bent over the other boy's motionless body. "You're as good as new. Up. Let's keep moving. Especially if there might be other, uh, *people* around."

Nick hadn't spent much time around Brenda, but she had always seemed so loving and generous and kind. She was pretty, too, with her long, curly red hair, and Nick liked her hippie-mom, easygoing approach to things. But now even she sounded suspicious and paranoid and scared.

Jackson sat up, swaying slightly. And then, as soon as his mother let go of him, he plummeted back toward the ground.

"Brenda!" Michael shouted. "Catch him!"

It was too late. Jackson was already flat on the ground, passed out again.

"Mom!" Ava cried. "I thought you said he was good as new!"

"Shh," Nick's own mom said, glancing around as if she expected Lida Mae and a whole crowd of suspicious cave dwellers to materialize out of the cave walls. "Let's not be shouting about Jackson's . . . limitations."

Ava sniffed, and Nick saw his dad put his arm around the girl. Michael went to kneel beside Jackson and Brenda, who seemed to be reaching into the boy's stomach again. Nick was glad he was standing too far away to see much. But he heard Brenda say in a hushed voice, "See, this wire is so frayed from us fixing him all the time, I bet it's going to keep coming loose. We can solder it for now, but . . ."

"But that's just a temporary fix," Michael muttered. "I'll have to leave the nature preserve tomorrow and get replacement parts."

"You should take Jackson with you," Brenda whispered.

Nick felt a hand clutch his arm. It was Eryn. He turned and met his sister's eyes. She raised an eyebrow, and the two of them started inching backward, away from the adults and Ava and Jackson. They didn't stop until they were at the outer edge of the glow of the nearest flashlight.

"If Brenda wants Jackson out of the nature preserve tomorrow . . . ," Eryn began, whispering into Nick's ear.

"Then she's more afraid of Lida Mae's family finding out he's a robot than anything else," Nick finished for her.

Eryn nodded. It was eerie looking at his sister in such near-total darkness. The shadows cast by her eye sockets made it look like she didn't even have eyes, just dark pits.

Stop freaking yourself out, Nick told himself. *Eryn's the one you trust!*

This wasn't comforting when his next thought was, *She's the only one I can trust.*

Eryn stood on tiptoes again to reach Nick's ear.

"What if Lida Mae or her family were the ones who wrote the papers from the desk in the secret room?" she asked. "What if it's not even true, it's just them being . . . prejudiced . . . against civilization? Against robots?"

Nick bent toward Eryn and felt the papers under his shirt stab into his skin. Were they full of lies or nothing but the truth?

Either way they were dangerous, and he and Eryn

sheepishly. Something teased at the back of his mind—
the memory of the papers he'd seen Nick stuff under
his shirt the night before. The ones with the horrifying
instructions on them. Maybe he should tell Dad about
them, now that they were away from Nick and Eryn. But
just thinking the word "papers" made his knees go weak
and his head spin.

*I'll think about this after Dad gets my replacement
parts, after all my internal links are good again,* Jackson
told himself. *I've got plenty of time. Nothing's going to
happen.*

Even thinking *that* made his vision blur. He reso-
lutely narrowed his eyes and gazed at the leafless trees
lining the trail, then at the low, gray sky overhead. He
thought about nothing but sky, trees, dirt. Nature. Once
everything came into focus again, he peered back at Dad.

"What I'm asking is, why am I the one who keeps
breaking down, when Ava almost never does?" Jackson
asked. "It's our programming, isn't it? How'd you design
us differently?"

Dad sighed. He usually didn't like to talk about his
kids' programming. He usually tried to pretend as much
as possible that they were totally human . . . just with
robotic bodies. He took a cautious glance around and

lowered his voice, as if he worried that there might be some creature more advanced than a squirrel within earshot. Someone who could eavesdrop.

"The differences . . . well, you're male and she's female," Dad began.

Jackson tried to decide if saying, *Well, duh, I knew that!* would earn him a lecture about being respectful or a proud grin because he sounded like a typical human kid. Before Jackson could make up his mind, Dad sighed again.

"My goal was to make the two of you seem like typical human kids from the early twenty-first century," Dad said. "And Denise explained to me that the gender stereotypes of that time left boys less room to express their emotions than girls. So it would appear that whenever you get emotional, you blow your circuits."

This time Jackson said, "Duh!" without thinking about it. "Dad, I know how it *feels*," Jackson added. "I just want to know how to fix it. How to . . . be chill."

"Some of it's just a matter of growing up," Dad began. "Getting through adolescence. Figuring yourself out. If it makes you feel any better, I'm sure generations of fathers and sons have had this same conversation. Or something like it."

"There haven't *been* generations of fathers and sons like *us*, Dad," Jackson muttered. "You don't know what it's like. Because you've never been a kid."

His father had been a middle-aged adult since the day he'd rolled off the assembly line. That was how it was with all the adults—they weren't designed to grow and change. Neither were the robot kids aged thirteen and over. As far as Jackson knew, he and Ava were the only robot kids ever who had started out as babies and gone through all the same developmental changes a human would go through in the first twelve years of life. In the beginning, Mom and Dad had even passed them off as human children—"to see if it could be done," Dad had said.

Until recently, Jackson had been as thrilled as Mom and Dad about fooling everyone.

In the past several months, though, when he began falling apart all the time, he'd started wondering, *Would it be so awful to just tell everyone what we are? So they'd understand that I'm not just . . . weird?*

Then Mom and Dad had broken it to him that telling anybody what he was would be deadly. Everything about him and Ava was illegal—there weren't supposed to be *any* robots who grew and changed. And there weren't supposed to be any robots their age; the rules were that only humans were supposed to have been born in the past twelve years.

That was why Mom had started homeschooling them, once Jackson and Ava began having trouble hiding their true nature.

And now that was part of the reason Mom and Dad and Denise and Donald had brought them all to this nature preserve, where nobody else was supposed to find them.

So how was it that Ava, Eryn, and Nick said some strange girl had shown up in the cave last night, even as Jackson lay passed out on the cave floor?

"Dad, do you think that girl saw me fall apart last night?" Jackson asked. He was afraid the question would send him into another breakdown. But he managed to keep striding forward along the trail. To keep pretending he didn't have a knot of worry eating away at his stomach. "What do you think would happen if—"

"Now, now, let's leave the unbridled speculation to the humans," Dad said. "We Lightner men deal in facts, remember? And as much as this is a run for parts for you, this is also a run for information."

Jackson inhaled sharply.

"You're going to risk an all-call request on the robot network, aren't you?" he asked. "Once we're back in range . . ."

As long as they were in the nature preserve, the four adults were cut off from the network of all the other robots in the world. Because if they had access to the knowledge of other robots, other robots also had the right to seek access to what they knew. For twelve years Mom and Dad—and, it turned out, the other two parents, Denise and Donald—had kept Ava and Jackson secret by acting so boring that no one ever wanted to probe their minds. But Nick and Eryn had drawn a lot of attention to the family recently, and the adults had decided they all needed to go into hiding.

Jackson had been watching the grown-ups since they got to the nature preserve. They all seemed stupider somehow, bumbling around without any knowledge except what was already in their own heads.

Jackson and Ava, being illegal, had of course never been allowed to link to the robot network. But Jackson daydreamed about it.

To know anything I want to know, anytime I want to know it? he thought. *How cool would that be?*

"Dad . . . what if I did the all-call instead of you?"

Jackson asked. "We could download the link into my mind and then—"

"What? *No!*" Dad exploded. "That's crazy! Do you *want* to get caught?"

"No, listen, it makes sense," Jackson said. He stopped on the trail and turned to face Dad. Dad started to breeze on by, but Jackson grabbed his arm and held him in place. "If you give your ID number for your all-call, which you'd have to do, your request would be grouped together with everything else you've ever asked. You've already got a pattern of questions that look suspicious. This one could be the tipping point, the one that makes law enforcement start looking at you. Examining your record. I don't have any record, any pattern. Anything I ask would just look like a random question from a random kid."

"You don't even have an ID number!" Dad protested. "You'd set off even more suspicions!"

"So we make one up," Jackson said. His knees felt weak again, but he ignored them. "We say I'm thirteen and perfectly legal. No one would know any different."

"Until it comes time for . . ." Dad's face contorted, and he jerked his arm out of Jackson's grasp. "Really, Jacky, you don't know what you're asking. You are not using a fake ID number to tap in to the network, and that's final!"

He called me Jacky? Jackson thought. *Like I'm five years old again? I give him a serious suggestion—a* mature, *thought-out suggestion—and he treats me like a little kid?*

Dad had started walking again, taking long, furious strides that kicked up dead leaves and gravel. Jackson still stood frozen on the trail. He could barely stand, let alone walk. Dad was several paces ahead before he stopped and turned around.

"Oh, Jacky," he murmured, shaking his head. He rushed back, calling, "Tell me, what's 4,208 times 9,306?"

It was a relief for Jackson to let such an easy question flow through his brain.

"That would be 39,159,648," he said automatically.

"And the square root of 6,486?" Dad asked, gently taking Jackson's arm and propelling him forward.

They did math problems the rest of the way down to the van. But Dad didn't know exactly how fast Jackson had made his processing speed. In between spouting numbers, Jackson had time to think:

Someday. Someday I will tap in to the robot network. And Dad won't be able to stop me.

FIVE

Eryn

Eryn bit into a granola bar that was so cold and hard she almost broke a tooth. She scowled at the gray clouds, which seemed to glower back at her from low in the sky, and she thought, *Hot chocolate. Cinnamon-apple oatmeal. Pancakes with butter melting on top . . .*

It was definitely a day for a hot breakfast. Even weak tea boiled over an open flame would have lifted her spirits after her night of tossing and turning—and worrying—as she tried to sleep on the cold ground with only dead, decaying leaves for a blanket.

But the adults had decided it was too risky to light another fire. Not when they didn't know exactly how nearby Lida Mae's family might be. Or—though the adults didn't say this—when they didn't know exactly how dangerous Lida Mae's family might be.

I bet Lida Mae's family has figured out geothermal heating, Eryn thought grumpily. *I bet they're sitting around all toasty and warm, drinking cocoa and not even thinking about us, while we're sitting out here in the cold worrying about them.*

But what if Lida Mae's family *was* thinking about Eryn's? What might they be thinking?

"Jumping jacks," Mom said from behind Eryn.

"What?" Eryn said, turning to glare at Mom.

"It's a known fact that exercise will get your blood flowing," Mom said briskly. "If you're cold, you need to move around more. Studies show that something something percent of something, uh . . . proves this."

Eryn lowered her granola bar and gaped at her mother.

"Did you just say 'something something percent of something' instead of quoting an actual statistic?" she asked incredulously.

Mom brushed a lock of Eryn's dark hair off her face.

"Don't look at me like that," she muttered. "I guess I never actually, uh, downloaded the exact statistic from the general robot network into my own brain. But I'm pretty sure there is a statistic about that. Maybe."

It wasn't like Mom to admit she didn't know something. Or to say "uh." Or "maybe." Or to focus on Eryn's appearance when Mom's own normally sleek, business-like bob was sticking out all over the place.

Or to sleep in the woods or run away from civiliza-tion or . . .

There wasn't time to keep listing all the things Mom had done for the first time in the past week, after that fateful day when Nick and Eryn decided to spy on their stepsiblings and found out way more than they ever expected.

Eryn glanced to the side, where Nick was coming up the hill from the makeshift bathroom Dad and Michael had built.

"Fine," Eryn told Mom. She tried to sound casual, like she didn't have a care in the world. "I'm game for exercise. Maybe Nick and I will take a hike this morning."

Would Mom fall for this? Or would Eryn have to explain why she wanted to hike—and what they'd be looking for?

"I don't want the two of you wandering off by your-self," Mom said. "Neither of you have had adequate preparation in wilderness survival training. It's too dangerous."

"But—" Eryn began.

"We're going to split up into two groups, with at least one adult in each group," Mom said. "And we'll do this systematically, and divide up the territory so we don't duplicate efforts."

"Do *what* systematically?" Eryn asked.

Mom cast a quick glance over her shoulder, as if she feared being overheard. But Dad was several yards away, whittling a branch down to be the support for a new, sturdier lean-to. Ava and her mother, Brenda, were eating their granola bars over by the ashes of the cold, burned-out fire, as if they thought there might be some hint of warmth left.

"You know," Mom said conspiratorially. "Look for that girl and her family. Assess them as risks."

Somehow it sounded worse to hear Mom say this. To have Mom admit that Lida Mae and her family might be a risk. Especially when Mom didn't even know about the papers from the secret room, or Eryn's suspicion that someone from Lida Mae's family might have written them.

Eryn stood up, looking at the last part of her granola bar in distaste. She reared back her arm to throw it out into the woods. As far as she was concerned, some bird or squirrel or chipmunk was welcome to it.

Mom caught Eryn's arm.

"Don't waste that," she warned. "Eat it—you'll need

the calories. And . . . we need to conserve our food. We don't know if we'll have enough for however long we need to stay out here."

Eryn lowered her arm and stared at Mom. Mom shook her head sternly and walked over to talk to Dad.

"What's going on?" Nick asked, coming up beside Eryn.

"Mom's gone loony tunes," Eryn said. "Being out in the woods is making her weird."

"Don't you mean, weird*er*?" Nick joked.

A week ago Eryn would have rolled her eyes and grinned at that. Today she could only cross her arms and shiver miserably. Why did being cold make her feel so discouraged?

Even Nick didn't seem to be able to muster a grin. His face stayed grim. Eryn glanced down toward the midsection of the coat he'd pulled on when they got back to the campsite last night. Did Nick still have the papers from the secret room tucked inside his shirt, under the coat, or had he moved them to some safer place, like a pocket? Was Mom far enough away now that Eryn could remind Nick to put them somewhere safe? And then maybe talk about what Nick and Eryn should do with them?

No, probably not, Eryn decided.

"Let's deal with Dad this morning, not Mom," Nick said. "Let's go tell him we want to go scout around for, um . . . what can we say to keep him from asking questions?"

"Mom says we're all going out searching after breakfast," Eryn told him glumly. "In groups. We've just got to make sure you and I are in the same group. What do you bet she'll want to make it girls in one group, guys in another?"

"We'll tell her that's discrimination," Nick said.

Eryn was about to say, *You know they won't agree to it being all robots in one group, just us in the other,* when she felt someone tap her on the shoulder.

How could that be, when Mom and Dad were still over by the lean-to, and Ava and Brenda were still by the fire? And Jackson and Michael should be halfway back to the van by now?

"I swear, you're huddled up like you're freezing half to death," a twangy voice said behind Eryn. "Want me to show you'uns how to build a fire that'll stay lit this time?"

Eryn spun around, even though she was dead certain who she'd see:

It was Lida Mae again.

SIX

Nick

"Um, uh . . . sure!" Nick said, because Eryn seemed to have lost the ability to speak. "That's really nice of you when we, uh . . ."

Eryn elbowed him in the ribs, a deep, painful jab. Even though Eryn always claimed she and he had spooky twin skills that allowed them to read each other's minds, Nick couldn't tell what this elbow nudge was supposed to mean. Was it *Argh! Did we say anything about robots that Lida Mae might have overheard?*

Maybe it was *Don't ask her any questions that will make her run away again! Be careful!*

Or maybe it was *Remember, don't let her see the papers you grabbed from the secret room ordering you to kill robots! Make sure you keep them hidden!*

Nick patted the top left section of his coat, where he could feel the folded-up lump of papers he'd tucked into an inner pocket. This was so much more secure than trying to hold them under his shirt.

Lida Mae squinted curiously at him and tilted her head, making her braids look lopsided.

"Oh, is that what you do instead of shaking hands, where you come from?" she asked. "Well, then . . ."

She patted the left side of her collarbone, aiming the gesture at first Nick, then Eryn. Lida Mae was wearing a heavy coat this morning that looked like its outer layer was homespun—some kind of burlap, maybe?—and her motion set off a little puff of dust.

Eryn coughed.

"That's not really a . . . common custom," she said faintly. "Just a Nick thing."

Now Eryn's face was squinched up and bright red. Nick couldn't tell if she was about to explode into laughter or screams. Or if she was just cold.

He decided to stop worrying about what Eryn might be thinking and figure out what he himself should say to Lida Mae.

"It's nice of you to try to adapt to my, um, custom," he said. "Do people in your family just shake hands when you greet each other?"

Lida Mae shook her head, sending her braids flying side to side. They thumped against her shoulders.

"Oh, no—we *hug*," she said. She grinned, revealing big white teeth that met at odd, whimsical angles. "But I don't know you that well. Yet."

Nick felt his own face turn red. Was she *flirting* with him?

"We would like to get to know you and your family better," Eryn said. Nick could tell she was picking her words carefully. "I mean, if that's okay with you."

She elbowed Nick again, and he was pretty sure what she meant this time.

"I'm sorry if I offended you last night, asking to see your family's farm," he said. "Maybe in your customs that was a terrible thing to do. I didn't mean to be rude."

Lida Mae grinned merrily again.

"My mammy says a true gentleman would *never* invite himself over to the abode of a girl he was courting," she said. "He lets her do the choosing of when it's time to meet her family."

It took Nick a moment to figure out her odd wording. It took him another moment to get over the shock.

"You think . . . you think I was asking because I want to be your boyfriend?" he asked. Eryn cleared her throat beside him, and Nick scrambled to add, "I mean, not that you're not really pretty and all, and you seem really smart, and . . ."

Lida Mae gave his shoulder a playful shove. Her hand hit just an inch above where she might have been able to feel the folded-up papers through his coat.

"Oh, I'm just joshing with you, of course," she said, giggling. "I'm only twelve, and you don't look any older, and that is much, much too young to think about serious courting. We'd have to be fourteen, at least."

Was she still joking with him?

If you didn't count Eryn, Nick hadn't been any good at talking to girls back home at school, back when things were normal. He *really* wasn't any good at it now.

Eryn rescued him, taking a slight step forward that put her closer to Lida Mae and let him take a little step back.

"About that fire you were offering to help us build," Eryn said. "Really, I think our parents know how to do that. They just let the fire go out because we're all about to take a hike, and we didn't want to start a forest fire or anything while we were away. Would you mind showing us around instead? Helping us find the best hiking trails?"

Not bad, Eryn, Nick thought admiringly.

Except hadn't their stepfather, Michael, said this nature

preserve covered hundreds of thousands of acres? Couldn't Lida Mae take them on a miles-long hike that purposely avoided showing them anything they wanted to see?

"We're doing everything we can to be safe, but our parents aren't exactly nature people," he said. "If they did accidentally start a fire . . . your family doesn't live too close, do they? And your house isn't downwind from here, is it?"

Eryn squinted at him. He couldn't tell if she approved of his sneaky way of trying to get information, or if she thought he'd gone too far.

But Lida Mae just gave both of them playful shoves this time.

"Oh, law, listen to you, worrying about forest fires," she giggled. "You are a pair of tenderfeet, aren't you? There's no call to worry about fire spreading with the ground this damp, and all the woods around us still soaking from last week's snowfall. But about that hike—sure, I'll show you around!"

Tenderfeet, Nick thought. *Joshing. Courting.*

Was Lida Mae really as folksy and backwoodsy and innocent as she seemed?

Or was she acting and pretending and hiding just as much as Nick and Eryn?

SEVEN

Ava

"Deep breaths," Mom murmured from behind Ava, where she'd moved to pull Ava's hair back into a tight, secure ponytail. "Stay calm."

Ava winced. As a robot designed to look as much as possible like a human, of course she could make herself appear to breathe more deeply. But it didn't actually help.

Maybe it didn't actually help humans, either.

"Mom, do *not* say, 'Don't fall apart,' because you know that makes it *more* likely that I'm going to break down," Ava muttered back. "I *see* that that girl is over there talking to Eryn and Nick, and I'm fine; I'm staying centered. I just need quiet so I can focus on staying centered. . . ."

"Good girl," Mom said as she patted Ava's back. Then she fell silent.

Finally, Ava thought.

Really, she needed the silence so she could listen to

Nick and Eryn and Lida Mae. They stood at the edge of the clearing, far enough from the log where Ava and Mom were sitting that they undoubtedly thought no one could hear them. But Ava could, easily.

Did Lida Mae just say something about "courting"? Ava thought. *Seriously?*

She wished she were at the right angle to see Nick's face—it was probably a masterpiece of adolescent-boy embarrassment. Even the back of his neck had gone red, at least in the quarter inch Ava could see in the gap between his coat collar and his hairline.

Ava shifted to studying Lida Mae's face: the wide, friendly hazel eyes; the sprinkling of cinnamon-colored freckles across her nose; the endearingly crooked teeth revealed with every generous smile.

If I designed someone to look trustworthy and likable, I'd make her look just like Lida Mae, Ava thought.

But of course that was crazy, because Lida Mae hadn't been "designed." She was clearly human, a random mix of inherited traits, just like Nick and Eryn.

Only it's genes and *environment that shape humans,* Ava reminded herself. *And if Lida Mae is telling the truth, her environment has always been very different from Nick and Eryn's. . . .*

Thanks to Ava's enhanced hearing and vision, she had probably noticed Lida Mae striding through the woods a full five minutes before Nick and Eryn saw her—or before Lida Mae herself knew she was being watched. The girl took such big steps, carefree and loose-limbed, not like anything Ava had seen before. Lida Mae could do that even in the long dress she was wearing today over some leg-encasing undergarment—long johns? Bloomers? Ava didn't usually associate those kinds of clothes with freedom.

Maybe it's because she's a human who's actually been raised by humans, Ava thought. *All the humans I've ever met before were raised by robots. It's got to rub off a little.*

Lida Mae's eyes darted toward Ava's, as if the other girl wanted to be her friend just as much as she wanted to be Nick's and Eryn's. Under the guise of tilting her head back so Mom could gather hair for the ponytail, Ava gave Lida Mae a quick nod and hoped the girl got the message: *Oh yeah, I'd love to be talking with you right now too. It's just my annoying mom keeping me here. . . .*

But once Mom finished, how would Ava justify not going over there to talk? Ava felt perfectly calm just listening; she wasn't sure she could hold on to that calm if she had to interact. And it would take Mom just an instant to wrap a rubber band around Ava's ponytail.

Oh, yeah . . .

"Mom, could you braid my hair instead?"

Out of the corner of her eye, Ava saw Mom turn her head and gaze briefly toward Lida Mae.

"Oh yes, imitation is the sincerest form of flattery. . . . Very smart. Good plan," Mom said, letting go of Ava's hair and reaching for a comb to part it into sections for braiding.

Ava had to turn sideways, which made it impossible to keep watching the other kids. But she kept listening, on and off. She also tuned in to the whispers behind her, where Nick and Eryn's parents, Denise and Donald, were conferring by the lean-to.

"Since that girl turned up again . . . do you think she secretly followed us back to the campsite last night?" Donald asked. "Do you think she lives close?"

"I don't know!" Denise said, her whisper tense and agonized. "I feel like I'm completely in the dark here—there's no security footage we can access, no information scan we can run. . . . I've never felt so clueless in my life. How do humans survive, feeling so ignorant all the time?"

"Denise, the sun did actually come up this morning," Donald said gently. "We're not literally in the dark."

Ava couldn't see behind her, of course, but she had the feeling Denise rolled her eyes at Donald.

"Michael will be back soon," Denise said. "Michael will have loads of information from the all-call. Then we'll know how to proceed."

She sounded so . . . reverent. She sounded like Ava's dad's coming back was the only hope she had.

"So in the meantime, are we just going to let Eryn and Nick do all the hard work of talking to that strange girl?" Donald asked. "A girl who . . . might be a threat?"

Is that what all the grown-ups think? Ava wondered. *My parents too?*

"Right now I trust Nick and Eryn to deal with her more than I trust myself," Denise said grimly. "I couldn't . . . I don't . . . Do you suppose this is how Jackson feels right before he falls apart?"

"Maybe you just have a wire loose, like Jackson did last night," Donald said. "We'll have Michael take a look at all our circuitry once he's back."

"What if I need to function properly before that?" Denise demanded. "What if our children's lives depend on me being able to make the right decision in an emergency situation *this morning*? What if everything we've ever worked for—"

She broke off so abruptly, Ava had to know what had happened. Ava jerked her head around, even though it meant messing up Mom's braiding.

"Ava!" Mom complained, grasping for dropped strands of Ava's red hair.

Ava ignored her and peered toward the other adults. Oh. Nick and Eryn were leading Lida Mae toward their parents, as if they planned to introduce her.

"Mom," Ava said softly. "I think we need to go help Donald and Denise. So they don't mess this up."

Ava liked it that Mom didn't say, *What makes you think we wouldn't mess things up even worse?* Or *But you haven't been functioning properly. I'll go. You stay here.* Instead she muttered, "Got it," and quickly wrapped a rubber band around Ava's hair, even though that left one pigtail braided all the way down to the tip, the other only halfway down.

Sometimes Mom could be kind of amazing at figuring out Ava.

Ava and Mom stood up and walked to the lean-to, reaching it just as the other three kids sidled up to Nick and Eryn's parents.

Denise looked pale. Donald ran a hand through his curly dark hair, making it look like he'd just barely survived a harrowing experience in a wind tunnel.

You can do this, Ava told herself. *You have to. Because the adults are losing it. And Nick and Eryn don't know what they're doing.*

She stuck out her hand to Lida Mae.

"Hi," Ava said brightly. "It's great to see you again. I'm Ava, if you don't remember from being introduced in the cave last night. It was so dark and a little bit scary in there . . . I'm not sure any of us remembered our manners exactly. Of course, you're probably used to that cave, but this is all new to us."

Ava didn't like to think about how Dad had programmed her—she didn't like to think about being "programmed" at all. But her chatterbox skills did come in handy sometimes.

Lida Mae pumped Ava's hand up and down, the most vigorous, enthusiastic hand shaking Ava had ever received.

"If you'uns stay around long, don't worry—I'll have you running up and down these hills and in and out of that cave like you were born to it," Lida Mae said.

"But . . . there are signs on the outside of the cave,"

Denise said weakly. "About how it's not safe to go in. Because of rockslides and sinkholes. We were there last night only because Eryn and Nick disobeyed. I . . . I don't want my kids to go back there. I forbid it."

Ava remembered that one of the signs in the cave— the one on the door to the secret room—didn't actually say that it was a dangerous area. It just said that no *robots* were allowed to enter the room. The adults had been able to defy their programming and enter only because they were motivated by a higher cause: the fear that their children were in danger.

Ava and Jackson had been able to enter because Dad had programmed them not to think of themselves as robots.

Has Lida Mae seen that sign? Ava wondered. *Does she even know how to read? So does she know that robots exist? Has she been into the room and read the papers that Nick swiped, the ones that say . . .*

This was not the time to think about those papers. Not if she wanted to avoid toppling over every bit as dramatically as Jackson had last night.

Fortunately, Nick and Eryn were taking over the conversation.

"Mom, don't be all crazy protective like that!" Nick protested.

"Yeah!" Eryn agreed. "Lida Mae's, like, an experienced cave guide! I'm sure she knows what she's doing. She wouldn't take us anywhere that's not safe."

Lida Mae shrugged in a way that seemed both modest and knowledgeable, all at once.

"I've been roaming around that cave since before I could walk, and I've never been in the slightest bit of danger," she said. "Because my family taught me what to watch for. Before rocks start falling or a sinkhole opens, there are always signs—I don't mean the kind with words you can read, but the way the rock creaks, or the way the bats fly away. . . . You just have to pay attention. And I know how to. Your children would always be safe with me."

"The kind with words you can read," Ava thought. That wasn't quite an answer to her questions, but at least Lida Mae was aware of written words and reading.

"Oh, now I'm forgetting my manners, too!" Lida Mae said, with a friendly giggle. She reached out to shake hands with each of the adults. "I'm Lida Mae Spencer. Pleased to make your acquaintance."

"And this is my mom, Brenda Lightner, and my stepmom, Denise Stone Lightner, and Nick and Eryn's dad, Donald Stone," Ava said, pointing to each of them in turn, because they all seemed a little numb and sluggish. They did manage to shake hands.

"Well," Eryn said, "I guess it's kind of like we're neighbors now. We can take turns visiting back and forth. Next time you come by, we'll have a fire going, and we can offer you cocoa or something better than . . ." She looked down at a rocklike object clutched in her hand. Or, no, it was just the remains of her breakfast. "Better than a frozen granola bar."

Was that an opening for Ava to say, *Do you live close enough that it'd be easy for your parents to come by and visit too?* Or *Can you give us directions so we know how to get to your house, when it's our turn to stop by?*

Ava's head swam. She couldn't say either of those things—they were too close to Nick's question from the night before, the one that had made Lida Mae flee. But was there something else Ava could say that would chip off a little bit of information at time? Not enough to scare Lida Mae, but enough to give Ava and her family what they wanted?

Before Ava could speak, her mother suddenly murmured, "Neighbors? I know a poem about neighbors. It's by Robert Frost. It's about walls and fences, and how—"

"Mom!" Ava protested, giving her mother a stunned

stare. Why would she bring up that poem? Jackson and Ava had puzzled over "Mending Wall" in their language-arts class only last week. It had a couple of lines about how you needed good fences between neighbors, and Mom had admitted that it didn't make any sense to her, either. Because it sounded like Robert Frost didn't want people to be friends.

What if Lida Mae thinks Mom's trying to get her to leave? Ava wondered.

Mom's head reeled back and forth, and she swayed dizzily.

Oh no, Ava thought. *Is Mom having the same problems Denise was talking about?*

What if Mom had been saying "Deep breaths" and "Stay calm" to herself, not to Ava, when they were sitting back on the log?

Now everyone was staring at Ava, because she had protested so dramatically.

That's fine, Ava told herself. *I need to cover for Mom. I can handle it.*

"Sorry," Ava said, forcing out a fake-sheepish giggle. "Bad language-arts flashback there. Too much poetry analysis." She faked a shudder, too. "But maybe you have more fun than we do at school, Lida Mae?"

Oh, good for me! Ava thought. *That's a way to find out if she's learned to read!*

But Lida Mae just shrugged and said, "Oh, maybe. Some days, I'm sure."

There was an awkward pause. Ava noticed that Donald had started sweating.

It's, like, forty degrees out here! Ava thought. *Lida Mae's going to think he's sick, or . . .*

"Anyway, about that hike we were planning," Nick said, and fortunately, everyone turned in his direction. "Lida Mae offered to go with Eryn and me, and she really knows what she's doing, so Mom, Dad, we won't need you following us around like we're babies. . . ."

Had he also noticed the sweat on his father's forehead? Or would he be trying to get away from the grownups no matter what?

Because of the instructions on the papers? Ava let herself think. *Or because . . .*

Ava saw the three grown-ups wince, one after the other. And Ava could tell: The adults were going to let Nick and Eryn go off with Lida Mae. The adults didn't think they had any choice.

And what should I do? Ava thought. *Stay here, and maybe get a chance to tell Mom and Denise and Donald about the papers Jackson and I saw Nick tuck under his shirt last night? Or go on the hike and find out more from Lida Mae?*

Was that the choice? Or was it *Which group do I belong in? The group of robots or the group of kids?*

Donald wiped his forehead. Denise blinked and winced and blinked and winced. Mom kept opening and shutting her mouth without saying anything, like a dumbstruck guppy.

Lida Mae absolutely could not stay at the campsite when the adults were having so many problems. Especially if they got any worse. Ava had to take control.

"And I'll go too, to keep Nick and Eryn out of trouble," she said. "Thanks, Mom! Thanks, Denise! Thanks, Donald!"

She leaned in and kissed the cheek of each adult in turn. With her mouth next to her mother's ear, she whispered, "Sit down and *breathe*. You'll be fine. Tell the others."

Then she grabbed Lida Mae's arm and spun her away from the grown-ups.

"Where should we go first?" she asked.

EIGHT

Jackson

Dad took off running once the van came into view, partially hidden by a clump of trees.

"Dad, wait for me!" Jackson complained, struggling to keep up.

But Dad didn't stop. He didn't stop even once he reached the van.

"No connectivity," he muttered as he ran. "No connectivity, no connectivity . . . Aaaahhh! Connection!"

Dad stopped in a ditch between the last of the trees and the berm of the highway they'd driven on the day before. He tilted his head back and slowly rotated his body, his eyes half-closed, his arms raised like someone worshipping the sun.

The sun looked pretty wimpy this cold winter day—far off and pale and overshadowed by the thick gray clouds. Jackson knew it wasn't actually the sun Dad was so excited about.

"You found it?" Jackson asked. "The first spot where there's a link available?"

"Shh," Dad said. "I'm starting a scan."

His expression stayed blissful. Dad was tall and thin and bald—he looked like the kind of guy who made practical decisions and wore sensible shoes. He *was* that type of guy. Most of the time.

Jackson didn't think he'd ever seen his dad appear so ecstatic.

Jackson waited a moment.

"Have you found anything on the network about Lida Mae and her family?" Jackson asked, inching closer to Dad. "Or . . . anything else you wanted to know?"

Even though Jackson didn't have a connective link installed in his own brain, would he be able to sense the spot where the dead zone of the nature preserve ended and all that flow of glorious information began?

Not yet . . . not yet . . . not yet . . .

Jackson found himself standing right beside Dad in the ditch. It felt no different to him from standing in the woods.

Dad's eyelids fluttered as he slowly revolved—then they sprang open when he saw Jackson so close by.

"Jackson, *no*," Dad said, as if Jackson were a poorly

trained puppy. "You stay in the woods as long as possible, just in case."

He grabbed Jackson's arm and yanked him back to the safety of the trees. Then Dad hurried back to his glorious ditch. He turned his back on Jackson.

Jackson knew Dad was only trying to protect him. After all, if Jackson broke down in the ditch, there was a chance, however small, that Dad's own view of him could be accessed by any other robot, anywhere in the world. As Jackson understood it, that was how brutally efficient the robot network could be. That was why Dad had so much confidence that if there was any information out there about people living near Mammoth Cave, his all-call would find it.

But Jackson couldn't help feeling a little hurt by Dad's shoving him away.

Someday maybe Dad and I will be able to do all-call searches for information together, Jackson thought. *Someday I'll probably be better at them than he is. . . .*

Dad inched a little closer to the road, a little farther from Jackson.

"Please," Dad murmured. "Oh, please . . ."

Maybe Jackson wasn't supposed to hear that. Maybe

Dad thought he'd spoken softly enough that no one heard him.

And then suddenly Dad's shoulders slumped. His arms drooped; his head fell forward—he looked like he barely had enough energy to keep standing.

"Dad?" Jackson asked.

Dad turned, his eyes practically closed. He stumbled back into the woods, grabbing at random branches to keep from falling.

"There's nothing," Dad said. "Nothing about Mammoth Cave, nothing about people living in this area . . . How could there be no information at all?"

"Um . . . because someone's hiding it?" Jackson asked.

He waited for his father to say, *Oh, don't be ridiculous.* But Dad just raised one eyebrow and said nothing.

After a long moment Dad said, "What are we going to do now?" and it was awful how he sounded like he really didn't know.

"Aren't we going to the nearest town to get parts so you can fix my wires?" Jackson asked.

Could Dad actually have forgotten?

"Oh, right," Dad said. He shook himself and pulled

away from the tree he'd been holding on to. "I guess so."

Jackson turned toward the van. The passenger-side door barely opened, since it was wedged so tightly against the nearest tree. But Jackson managed to squeeze in. He shut the door and pulled on his seat belt.

Dad was still standing back by the tree, staring at Jackson.

Jackson rolled down the window.

"What are you waiting for?"

"No," Dad said in a choked voice. "That won't work."

"What are you talking about?" Jackson asked.

"We have to hide you better than that," Dad said. "We can't risk any mistakes. You can't sit there. We'll have to hide you in the back. Under a blanket, where no one will see."

"Are you crazy?" Jackson asked. "I didn't hide under a blanket yesterday, coming from Ohio. We were in this van for six hours, and I was in full sight of at least one window the entire time. Ava and I both were. What's changed since yesterday?"

Dad let his eyes close, and it seemed to take great effort to open them again.

"Everything," he murmured.

"But, Dad—"

"Jackson," Dad said, and now his voice was tender and loving. This was how Dad had sounded to Jackson when he was a little boy. "I'm trying to keep you alive."

How could Jackson argue with that?

I'm sure Dad was telling the truth about not learning anything about Mammoth Cave or people living nearby, Jackson thought as he opened the door again and started struggling around to the back of the van. *But . . . is there something else that he* did *find out? Something that's too horrible for him to tell me?*

NINE

Eryn

"If you're still here next fall, you are going to want to remember this spot," Lida Mae said, planting her feet in the exact middle of the trail. "There are pawpaw trees there, there, and there." She pointed at three leafless trees, though Eryn couldn't tell any difference between their bare branches and any others. "And eating pawpaws is like dying and going to heaven. Without the dying part, of course. Best fruit ever."

Next fall? Eryn thought.

"I'm sure—" she began.

"I'm sure these woods are beautiful in the fall," Ava interrupted.

Eryn had intended to say, *I'm sure we aren't still going to be here next fall.* Because it wasn't possible. Was it? Surely the grown-ups had planned to stay in the woods for only a week or so, until all the attention Nick and Eryn had gotten back home had blown over and everyone could go back to living normally, just keeping certain facts about Ava and Jackson secret, like always. The papers Nick and Eryn had found in the secret room complicated things, but once the kids were home again, maybe they could do some secret computer searches and solve the dilemma of the papers that way.

It was funny how, now that it was daylight, now that she'd walked a little, and now that she'd had breakfast (however pitiful), Eryn could see some fairly simple solutions to her problems.

She *longed* to be able to deal with the papers just by doing a few computer searches. Preferably while sitting in her own warm room at home (at either Dad's or Mom's house—it didn't matter which) with all the knowledge of civilization at her fingertips. From the first moment she'd laid eyes on the secret papers from the secret room, she'd been certain that there had to be some way out of the dilemma other than actually destroying all the robots in the world. A computer search could help her and Nick find that way, right?

If there's any way to keep that search secret, she thought.

And if they could figure out the mystery of Lida Mae, whose very existence seemed to defy everything Eryn had come to understand either from the robot adults she knew or from the messages left behind by the humans of the past.

Eryn grudgingly decided that she should be glad Ava had interrupted before Eryn could say something snobby or bitter about Lida Mae's woods. She didn't want Lida Mae running off again.

But having Ava along meant that Eryn and Nick couldn't just come out and say, *Lida Mae, have you seen the secret room in the cave with its secret papers talking about robots?*

Eryn wasn't sure she had the nerve for that anyhow.

What if she or Nick or Ava said something that scared Lida Mae away again, and they were left lost and far from the campsite? Something like *Are you descended from the people who wrote the papers we took from the secret room? Does that mean humanity didn't die out after all, so robots weren't as dangerous as everyone thought? So there's no need for Nick and me to destroy all the robots now?*

Those were the kinds of questions Eryn really wanted answered.

"How do you pick the . . . what are they called?" Nick asked. "Pawpaws? Is there some kind of machine you use?"

Oh, good try, Nick, Eryn thought. *Way to find out what kind of technology her family has! Way to inch toward the information we really want to know . . .*

It would only take about a million years to get there.

Lida Mae giggled.

"A pawpaw-picking machine? What a thought," she said. "Nah, you do it by hand. They fall to the ground when they're ripe—any machine would crush them. Though if you've got little brothers or sisters or cousins, *they're* good for picking up pawpaws. Being so low to the ground and all. That's kind of like having a picking machine."

"Do you have lots of little kids in your family?" Eryn jumped in.

"Oh, you know how it is with little kids," Lida Mae said with a vague wave of her hand. "One or two of them can seem like a dozen, the way they run around. Makes it hard to count."

Did Lida Mae even know how to count?

Eryn couldn't think of a way to ask that without sounding insulting.

They tramped on down the trail. As far as Eryn could tell, it looked no different from the trails they'd hiked the day before, coming from the road to their campsite:

dead leaves underfoot, dead-looking leafless trees on either side.

"What are we close to right now?" Eryn asked, trying to sound casual. "The cave? The cave entrance?"

Lida Mae snorted, sounding just as amused by Eryn's question as she'd been by Nick's.

"Mammoth Cave goes on for more than four hundred miles," she said. "And there are something like thirty entrances. It's right below us. You're on top of some part of the cave anywhere around here."

"Is it safe to walk on top of the cave?" Ava asked. "Is it safe to live here? Is anyone's house nearby?"

Is that too dangerous a question? Eryn wondered. *Too close to Nick's question that made Lida Mae run away last night?*

Lida Mae just shrugged.

"Cave's a long way down," she said. She grinned mischievously. "Don't worry—no one's going to fall through. Not even if you jump up and down and *try*. And we're not disturbing anyone, walking here."

That's not what Ava asked! Eryn wanted to scream. *This is impossible!*

She put her hand on Nick's arm and held him back as Ava and Lida Mae walked on. Once they were a few paces behind, she whispered, "She's got to start giving us better answers! So we have to start asking better questions! Harder questions that might make her run away again . . . Would you be able to find a way back to the campsite if she did that?"

"Um. . . maybe?" Nick said, looking back down the trail. "Didn't we turn right and then left and then . . ."

Eryn was pretty sure it had been a left turn first.

"GPS would really help right now!" she fumed.

"But couldn't someone track us if we used GPS?" Nick asked.

By *someone*, Eryn knew he meant the robots outside the park. Every robot in the world, actually, since they were all linked.

"Wasn't that why Mom destroyed everyone's cell phones yesterday when we got to the nature preserve?" Nick went on. "Isn't that why the adults are avoiding the robot network, out here in the nature preserve, so we're all off the grid?"

"Yes," Eryn muttered.

"Do you think the adults are . . . okay . . . away from the network?" Nick asked. "Mom and Dad and Brenda all looked kind of sick when we left."

Eryn didn't like how that sounded: as if she and Nick

and Ava had just abandoned their parents when they needed help. What if the adults needed someone to take their temperature or bring them warm soup? Or . . .

Eryn realized she'd started thinking of her parents as human beings once again. Whatever need they had for soup—or any food—was just a pretense. Just a way they'd been designed to fool their children into thinking they were human. And Nick and Eryn had been completely fooled until the day they met Ava and Jackson, not even a week ago.

As far as Eryn knew, all the other humans in the world were *still* fooled. That would be all the other kids in the world who were twelve and under, except for Ava and Jackson.

And does that include Lida Mae and all her brothers and sisters and cousins? Eryn wondered. *Do they know about robots or not?*

Eryn just didn't know how to think about Lida Mae and her family. It always made her irritable not to know things. And the more she found and saw and experienced here in the nature preserve, the more clueless she felt.

"I'm sure the adults will be fine," she huffed to Nick.

Several paces ahead, Ava turned and peered back at Nick and Eryn.

"Are you two getting tired?" she asked. "Do we need to stop and take a break?"

"Sorry," Eryn said. "We're not tired. We were just being slow because . . ."

"Because we were looking at all the different kinds of leaves on the ground," Nick finished for her.

Eryn flashed her brother an *I owe you one* look. She just hoped Ava and Lida Mae didn't notice.

"Lida Mae's been telling me how some of the vegetation around here can be used for medicine. And some can be food that tastes a lot better than you'd think," Ava said, making it sound like she'd actually been interested in hearing about trees.

Eryn didn't have the patience for this.

"You know what I was thinking?" she said, picking up her pace to catch up with Ava and Lida Mae. Nick trailed just a step or two behind her. "We're having this nice hike with you today, Lida Mae, but what if we want to hang out with you tomorrow or the next day or the day after that, and we haven't made plans ahead of time? Or what if we make plans, and then someone gets sick and needs to cancel?"

"How would we get in touch with you?" Nick finished for her, and she shot him another grateful look.

"Oh, goodness, we can make plans for all sorts of hikes and outings, any day you like," Lida Mae said. "We can plan all that ahead of time. I don't have to ask permission. Mammy and Pap let me roam anywhere I want, as long as I get my chores and lessons done each day. And don't worry—I almost never get sick."

That wasn't the point! Eryn wanted to shout.

"Back home we can communicate between, say, our house and the houses our friends live in, even if they're a long way away," Nick said, taking up the cause.

Oh, good grief, Eryn thought. *Is he going to suggest smoke signals between our campsite and wherever Lida Mae lives? Does he think it's worth it to work so hard to get one little scrap of information, like what direction Lida Mae lives in, starting from the campsite?*

That would be more useful information than they'd gotten out of Lida Mae so far. Maybe they could work up from there to talking about text messages and e-mail and computers . . . and robots.

"Oh, you mean, you use a telephone?" Lida Mae asked.

"You know what a telephone is?" Eryn asked, gaping at the other girl. "Do you have one?"

Lida Mae rolled her eyes and smirked.

"Now, what need would my family have for a tele-phone, when they don't have any desire to go contacting the outside world?" she asked.

"To talk to, uh, your aunts and uncles and cousins in their houses?" Eryn asked.

"Now, that's just silly," Lida Mae scoffed. "Why would we need a phone when my whole family all lives so close to each other we can just drop by anytime we want?"

"That's the kind of thing we mean," Ava said, smiling sweetly. "*We* can't do that. Because we don't want to be rude, of course, but also . . ."

Don't say it! Eryn thought at Ava. *Don't say, "Because we don't know where you live," because that's going to scare her away again!*

"Well, actually, we could use these," Lida Mae said, reaching into a pocket of her skirt and pulling out a palm-size object. "I was going to offer this later, but now's as good a time as any. Have you ever seen a walkie-talkie before?"

TEN

Nick

Ms. Girl Who Dresses Like It's the 1800s is asking us *if we've ever seen a walkie-talkie?* Nick thought.

Then he got a good look at the object in Lida Mae's hand. It wasn't like any electronic gear he'd ever seen. Rather than rubber or plastic, the outer covering of the walkie-talkie looked like walnut shells pieced together. The antenna looked like an old rusty nail bent into an arc.

Or maybe it was a miniature horseshoe.

"You're just playing with us, right?" Nick asked, before he had time to think. "No way that actually works."

Lida Mae's face flushed.

"Of course it does," she said. "Not inside the cave, usually, because you need more of an open range. But out here the signal can go for miles. Here. I'll prove it."

She handed Nick the walkie-talkie and pulled a second one from another pocket.

"Hold it up to your ear and listen," she said.

She ran a ways up the trail, rounding a curve so Nick could no longer see her.

Nick got a bad feeling in his stomach.

"Nick! Do what she says!" Eryn hissed at him, lifting his hand toward his ear and pressing her own ear toward the "walkie-talkie" too.

"See? Do you believe me now?" came rumbling out of the walnut-shell walkie-talkie. Lida Mae's voice was staticky and hard to understand, but the walkie-talkie definitely worked.

"Yes!" Nick called out to her, trying to throw his voice hundreds of feet ahead on the path.

"Press in the nailhead on the side and tell me that way," Lida Mae whispered back through the walkie-talkie.

Nick saw the nailhead she meant.

"You're right!" he said, in a reasonably normal voice. "You win!"

Eryn pulled his finger off the nailhead.

"How do walkie-talkies work?" she asked quietly. "Do *their* signals travel by satellite? Would anyone . . . outside . . . be able to hear Lida Mae's family using these? Or us?"

"Walkie-talkies use radio signals, not satellites," Ava said, like someone reciting a lesson in school. "Nobody could eavesdrop unless they were in range. Which means they'd have to be in this nature preserve to hear."

Eryn and Nick both stared at her.

"What?" Ava said. "I have a good memory. I know stuff like that."

"Never mind," Eryn said.

Nick realized it had been a few moments since Lida Mae had said anything over the walkie-talkie. And he couldn't see where she'd gone. He pressed the nailhead on the side again.

"Uh, Lida Mae?" he said, trying to keep the nervousness out of his voice. "You've proved your point. You can come back now."

Silence.

"Lida Mae?" he called again, shouting this time.

Birds chirped in the trees. The wind blew, ruffling the dead leaves on the ground. Lida Mae didn't answer.

"She wouldn't have gone off and left us just because Nick didn't believe her," Eryn said. "Would she?"

"Let's go catch up to her," Ava said.

They hustled up the trail, practically running. They rounded the curve that had made the rest of the trail disappear.

Lida Mae was nowhere in sight.

ELEVEN

Ava

Ava had strange thoughts sometimes.

Watching Nick talk back and forth with Lida Mae, she hadn't decided, *Oh, right, that means that primitive-looking walkie-talkie really does work. Amazing!* She'd thought, *How would Jackson and I fake something like that, if we wanted to fool Nick and Eryn, just for fun?*

She was pretty sure her own enhanced hearing would have allowed her to dash a half mile up the trail and hear anything Nick said, even if he spoke in a whisper. She and Jackson had played around with ventriloquism once—being homeschooled and trapped in the house with Mom all day sometimes made them desperate for entertainment. Ava hadn't had much talent for it, or liked it enough to keep practicing. But for a week or two Jackson constantly played pranks like pretending to yell from upstairs, "Ava! Get up here quick! You've got to see this!" when he was really hiding behind the couch. He only stopped when Ava confronted him: "Did you alter your voice box so you're transmitting by radio waves somehow, to be so good at that? You know, if Mom or Dad figure out what you've done, they may start examining all your circuits and find out what you did to your sight and hearing. And then—back to ordinary for you!"

But Jackson and I always try as hard as we can to seem like normal human beings anytime we're around humans, Ava thought. *For years our lives have depended on that. What's Lida Mae trying to prove? Or hide? Why would she want us to think her family has the technology to make walkie-talkies if they really don't?*

Ava reminded herself that, as far as she could tell, Lida Mae was human. Her eyes looked like human eyes, her movements were completely free of jerkiness—and she raved about pawpaws, of all things.

What if she and her family are humans who . . . evolved? Ava wondered.

She wasn't sure how many generations ago Lida Mae's family might have been cut off from the rest of humanity.

It had to have been before the rest of humanity ended, Ava thought grimly.

That was centuries ago. Was that enough time for

Lida Mae's family to have developed extreme hearing, along with the ability to throw their voices over a distance of a half mile? Ava tried to think scientifically: Would those adaptations be useful in and around Mammoth Cave?

It really was simpler to believe that Lida Mae and her family could build walkie-talkies out of walnut shells and rusty nails.

So why was Ava fighting against believing that?

Eryn tugged on Ava's arm.

"Do you think Lida Mae is coming back?" Eryn asked, clearly struggling to keep the panic out of her voice. "If we're stranded out here on our own, do *you* think we could find our way back to the campsite?"

"Probably," Ava said, answering both questions with one word. She flipped her uneven braids over her shoulders. The truth was, she would be able to make it back to the campsite blindfolded, because she and Jackson had both added some directional assistance to their brains, along with the other changes they'd made. But it was better not to reveal that unless she had to. "I think Lida Mae's just playing a prank on us. Or starting a game. Hide-and-seek, maybe?"

"Eryn didn't like hide-and-seek even when she was a little kid," Nick muttered.

"Is it wrong to want to know stuff for sure?" Eryn asked. "To not have things hidden?"

"Let's look around," Ava suggested. "Just . . . don't get lost."

Eryn picked up a stick and started poking it into the underbrush lining the trail. Nick peeked around tree trunks.

Ava looked up, toward the treetops.

That's where I'd hide, she thought. *Climb a tree, cling to a branch that's higher than anyone would expect a twelve-year-old girl to reach . . .*

Bingo.

There, high above the ground, Ava saw a flash of pale, freckled skin. Lida Mae's tan coat and brown boots and faded grayish skirt and long johns blended in with the tree she was hiding in and the cloudy sky beyond. But her face stood out.

Did Ava dare call out, *I see her!*? Or would that reveal too much about Ava at the same time it revealed Lida Mae's location?

It was so hard sometimes, trying to remember how little she was supposed to be capable of. Trying to remember what was "normal."

"Do you think Lida Mae might have figured out too much?" Eryn asked nervously. "Like, do you think she noticed our parents were acting strange back at the campsite? And maybe just now she realized that Ava is a—"

"Stop," Ava said, her voice sharp as a razor.

"If Lida Mae's hiding nearby, she can hear every word we say," Nick whispered.

Ava mouthed, *Thank you*, at him. Eryn flinched and muttered, "You're right. Sorry."

Was *that* maybe the reason Lida Mae was hiding? So she could eavesdrop on what they said when they thought she wasn't listening?

Ava let her gaze glide across the treetops as if she'd seen nothing unusual. She was careful not to pause at all or peer in Lida Mae's precise direction. But even her quick glance was enough to prove: Lida Mae had her head tilted. She was listening intently.

"Lida Mae!" Ava called. "This isn't funny anymore! We're getting scared!"

Out of the corner of her eye Ava saw Lida Mae start climbing down from her lofty perch.

"Sorry! Sorry!" she called back. "I didn't mean to

scare you! I was just checking on . . . I'll tell you when I get down there!"

"Where is she?" Eryn said from behind Ava.

Even with Lida Mae shaking the whole tree as she scrambled down, Eryn and Nick were still squinting hopelessly off into the distance, unable to pick out the movement.

Ava was glad she hadn't admitted she'd seen Lida Mae at the top of the tree, even farther away.

"Oh, there she is!" Nick finally said, long after Lida Mae had plopped to the ground and started fighting her way toward them through the underbrush.

Lida Mae was breathless by the time she reached the trail.

"Don't you feel the change in the air?" she asked. "The wind switched directions, and then I climbed a tree to see if I could pick out any other signs, off in the distance. . . . I kind of forgot about the walkie-talkies."

"What was so important that you could forget you were talking to Nick?" Eryn asked, a little huffily.

"There's a bad storm coming," Lida Mae said, her eyes wide and worried. "Maybe a blizzard. We've got to go prepare. You and your parents should move your campsite into the cave tonight, to stay safe."

Eryn and Nick gasped. Ava narrowed her eyes. Her brain was thinking differently once again.

Is there really a blizzard coming? she wondered. *Or is Lida Mae just telling us that to get us to all go back into the cave?*

But why would she want that?

TWELVE

Jackson

Dad's driving was jerky. Maybe it just seemed that way because Jackson was huddled under a blanket in the back of the van rather than safely seat-belted in. But it made Jackson worry. Did he dare to speak up? To yell at his father?

Dad, be careful! he could say. *If you mess up so badly that the cops stop you, what if they search the van? What if they find me?*

He was pretty sure police officers gave tickets to parents who didn't use seat belts on their kids. But that was the least of their worries.

Jackson didn't shout anything up to his dad about being cautious. Each jerk of the van made him more and more convinced that something was really wrong. Dad was already distracted enough.

Jackson's internal clock told him that they were on the highway for twenty-five minutes before Dad finally took an exit ramp. Then there was a series of stops and starts—for stop signs? Traffic signals?—before Dad came to a complete halt and turned the engine off.

"This is the nearest store to the nature preserve that has the electronic parts I need," Dad said, sounding almost casual, as if trying to give the impression he was only muttering to himself. "I'll just run in and run back out—it won't take a minute. And then I'll drive right back to the nature preserve."

Was that Dad's way of telling Jackson to just stay where he was?

Jackson didn't poke his head out from under the blanket. He heard Dad's car door open and close.

He waited.

And waited.

And waited.

This is "it won't take a minute"? Did he mean it won't take a minute because it will actually take an hour? Jackson thought grumpily.

He listened hard, catching sounds of distant traffic, chirping birds, and a flapping that was probably a flag blowing in a strong wind.

He didn't hear any footsteps, or anyone talking anywhere near the car. He dared to ease the blanket back, uncovering his eyes. From his position on the van floor he could see nothing through the windows but the gray, murky sky. Since no face appeared pressed against the glass, he gathered his courage and inched his head up to look out.

The van was at the back of a gravel parking lot, a good three rows away from any other vehicle. A deserted walkway led up to a low wooden building with a sign labeling it GENERAL STORE. And, as he'd suspected, a vast American flag hung on a tall flagpole out front. A strong wind whipped it back and forth.

I wish Ava and I had given ourselves X-ray vision, so I could see what's going on inside *that store,* Jackson thought.

He had considered it, but he hadn't seen any way to do it without changing his eyes so dramatically that Mom and Dad would have noticed.

What if Dad's having some problem, and he needs me to go in there and rescue him? Jackson wondered. *How would I even know?*

Just then he saw the door of the store swing open, banging the wall beside it. Dad stumbled out.

Jackson dove back under the blanket, even as his brain rang with the thought *Why did Dad stumble? Is he all right? Did something happen?*

From under the blanket he heard a door latch click, but the sound didn't come from the front of the van, up by the driver's seat. It was the latch of the door closest to Jackson that seemed to have released.

Was it Dad? Was he just putting his purchases in the back?

Or was it someone else?

Jackson heard ragged breathing. That didn't sound like Dad.

The door opened, and someone climbed past Jackson into the row of seats ahead of him. The door slammed shut.

"Quick! Let me download something into your brain. . . ."

It was Dad's voice.

Jackson rose up from the floor. Dad groped for the back of Jackson's head, where there was a small data port hidden in Jackson's hair. In the instant before Jackson turned, he caught a glimpse of Dad's twisted, anguished face.

"What's wrong?" Jackson asked. "Are you sick?"

Dad was never sick. Not for real. That was one of the benefits of being a robot.

An adult robot, anyway.

"No time . . . to explain," Dad muttered. "Just . . . do you have it yet? What I'm sending you?"

Jackson scanned his own mind. There it was, something new: a file labeled HOW TO DRIVE.

"What?" Jackson said. "*What?* You're teaching me how to drive *now*?"

"Have to," Dad mumbled, his words slurring together. "You have to drive back to the nature preserve. I'm shutting myself down. I—"

He collapsed against the van seat. Jackson's reached for his father's arm, to yank him back up, but the arm was limp and floppy. So was the rest of his body.

Dad had completely stopped functioning.

THIRTEEN

Eryn

Lida Mae led Eryn, Nick, and Ava back toward the campsite at a pace that practically could have set Olympic records. Eryn and Nick struggled to keep up; Ava didn't seem fazed.

Just like she was so calm when we thought Lida Mae had abandoned us, Eryn thought resentfully. *Just like she was so quick about distracting Lida Mae from noticing Mom and Dad and Brenda. . . . It must be nice to be a robot!*

She didn't really believe that. Robots were too artificial, too emotionless, too boring. Everything about them was programmed, and Eryn liked being able to think for herself. To make her own choices.

Right now, though, I wouldn't mind somebody else giving me a really good suggestion about how to deal with Lida Mae, and with the papers Nick swiped from the secret room, and with Mom and Dad acting so weird, and . . .

It didn't help to list everything Eryn was worried about. But if Mom and Dad and Ava's mother, Brenda, were still messed up—or possibly even getting worse— how could the kids keep Lida Mae from noticing once they got back to the campsite?

Eryn forced herself to pick up her pace and catch up with Lida Mae.

"Why don't you tell us now what we'll need to do to prepare for the storm?" she asked. "That way, once we get back to the campsite, we can handle telling our parents, and you can head back to your family as fast as possible to help them. We can, uh, call you on the walkie-talkie if we have any questions."

There, Eryn thought. *That will work. Won't it?*

Ava raced up alongside her and Lida Mae.

"Or, if your family needs a lot of help—getting your sheep safely into the barn, or whatever—then maybe some of us can go with you to deal with that work," she suggested.

Okay, got to hand it to you, Stepsis, Eryn thought. *That was a stroke of genius. Way to go! You really do sound like you want to help, not like you're just being nosy!*

But Lida Mae shook her head.

"Thanks for the offer, but my family has been through this so many times, we're fine on our own," she said. "Let's concentrate on keeping your family safe, since it's clear you'uns aren't really used to camping. Or being out in nature at all."

"Well, we *kids* aren't, but our parents know a lot more than we do," Nick said, pushing his way in to talk to the three girls.

Lida Mae seemed to be trying really hard not to roll her eyes.

"No offense, but I saw how they set up your campsite," she said. "I want to talk to your parents directly, to make sure they understand how serious this storm could be."

Of course you do, Eryn thought miserably. *I tried to prevent that, Ava tried, Nick tried . . . we all just struck out.*

She hadn't noticed anything odd about the weather when Lida Mae had first mentioned the change in the air. But the wind was picking up now, tugging violently at Eryn's shoulder-length hair and whipping it into her eyes. Eryn wished she'd had the sense to pull it back into a ponytail or do braids like Lida Mae's and Ava's. Though, now that she was paying attention, she noticed that Ava's pigtails were oddly done, the braiding ending only halfway down on the one side.

Is that another sign that the robots in my family are going loco? Eryn wondered. *Should Nick and I be most worried about* Ava *falling apart in front of Lida Mae?*

Lida Mae took a sudden turn onto a smaller trail. She led the other kids over a rise, and a sturdy-looking shed came into view.

"Oh, wow," Lida Mae murmured, coming to a halt. "Your parents got a lot done while we were hiking."

This is our campsite? Eryn marveled. *That shed is something Dad built? That's what his lean-to became? When we were only gone for a couple of hours?*

"Dad's job is building houses," Nick said, a hint of pride in his voice. "He's really good at building things."

"And fast," Lida Mae agreed.

Too fast? Eryn worried. *Is that shed going to make Lida Mae realize there's something really weird about my family?*

Dad stepped out of the shed.

"Oh, you guys are back already!" he called, giving

a broad, welcoming wave. "How was it? Bracing wind, don't you think?"

The wind made his wild, curly hair dance all over the place, but messy hair was normal for him. He wasn't sweating anymore either. Maybe he was okay again.

Lida Mae strode purposefully toward him and the shed.

"Mr. Stone, I need to talk to you'uns about that wind," she said. "Are the other grown-ups around?"

"The women are," Dad said. "Michael—that's Ava's dad—he's not back yet, but I'm sure he'll be coming soon." A hint of worry crossed his face, but he replaced it with a smile quickly enough that maybe Lida Mae didn't notice. He held open the rough door of the shed—it was amazing that the shed even had a door. "Please, come into our humble dwelling."

He wouldn't invite Lida Mae in to talk to Mom and Brenda if they weren't fine now too. Would he? Eryn wondered.

She and Nick and Ava trailed after Lida Mae. It was crowded and dim inside the shed, but Eryn saw Mom and Brenda stacking rocks against one wall, as if they were putting together the base of a fireplace.

That was bizarre. As far as Eryn knew, Mom had never built anything in her life. In fact, for years she and Dad had said they got divorced because Dad liked working with his hands and Mom just liked thinking.

Of course, now Nick and Eryn knew there was a lot more to the story.

But Mom and Brenda both looked normal enough as they stood up, smiled, and greeted Lida Mae much more warmly than they had before.

"I'll get right to the point," Lida Mae said. "There's a blizzard coming, and even though your shed is really amazing for a morning's work, it's not going to give you enough protection against the kind of wind and snow we're likely to get. Or the cold."

Eryn saw all the grown-ups exchange glances.

"We were about to put mud between those logs," Dad said. "Now that we have the kids here to help too, we—"

Lida Mae shook her head.

"There's no time for that," she said. "Not when you can just weather the storm inside the cave. That's so much safer."

"But the KEEP OUT signs," Mom said. "The . . . the danger of rockslides and sinkholes . . ."

Can't you give that a rest, Mom? Eryn thought impatiently. But she knew Mom probably couldn't.

"I'll tell you the best place to go in the cave," Lida Mae said. "You'll be fine. And in the cave you won't get frostbite, or lose your fingers or toes. Or freeze to death."

Did Lida Mae have to be quite so blunt? Eryn knew that Mom wasn't just scared of rockslides and sinkholes. There was also the problem of how she and all the other robots were programmed. All the grown-up robots, anyway. They really *couldn't* disobey a KEEP OUT sign, unless they had to, to protect their children.

"Don't worry, Mom," she said. "Nick and I—and, I guess, Ava—we'll go in first. So you'll have to follow us, to make sure we're safe."

Was she too obvious, saying that in front of Lida Mae?

But Lida Mae nodded, muttering, "Yes, that's what my parents are like too. Always putting their kids' needs ahead of their own."

"Were you planning to stay here to help us?" Ava asked, in a tremulous voice that really did make her sound scared. "Don't let us keep you. We know you have your own family to worry about."

"Yes, yes . . . ," Lida Mae said vaguely. "I'll go check

on my family, and then I should be able to come back to help you before the worst of the storm hits. But don't wait for me. Start moving your food and other supplies into the cave now. . . ."

She kept talking, giving instructions, but Eryn barely listened. She was too busy watching Mom, Dad, and Brenda and trying to figure out how they suddenly seemed like themselves again.

And then Lida Mae was saying her good-byes and final warnings and pushing her way out the door into the wind, which seemed stronger than ever.

It blew the door shut with a bang as soon as Lida Mae let go of it.

Ava peeked out through the cracks in the shed, as if she wanted to make sure Lida Mae was really truly gone.

"Is there *any* way to get in touch with Dad and Jackson?" she asked. "So we can warn them, too?"

Was that what she'd been so worried about? Eryn wondered. *Jackson and his dad are robots! What danger would a blizzard be to robots? It's not like they could get frostbite or lose their fingers or toes. Or die.*

That made her feel so much more vulnerable, as a human. She caught Nick's eye, and he gave her a grim nod. At least she wasn't the only human around.

Brenda moved over and put her arm around Ava's shoulder.

"No, we can't get in touch with your dad or Jackson, but once Dad left the nature preserve and linked into the robot network, he was bound to hear a weather report," she said. "He'll know to take appropriate precautions."

Would that mean staying outside the nature preserve, where Jackson might be discovered if he breaks down again in some dramatic way? Eryn wondered.

She decided not to ask that question out loud.

"Was Michael . . . acting normal when he left?" Nick asked. "Or was he sweating, or having trouble talking, or . . ."

Good question, Eryn thought.

"He was doing reasonably well," Mom said defensively. "And all the evidence we can gather would seem to indicate that once he was back in touch with the wider robot network, any dysfunctional symptoms he might have shown would have disappeared."

Okay, Mom's feeling fine again, Eryn thought. *Back to using ten big words where a few smaller ones would work just as well.*

"Can you translate that into normal English?" she asked.

"Once he's off the nature preserve, Michael should be back to normal," Dad said. "It was just inside the nature preserve that he might have had problems. Like the rest of us."

"Because we weren't designed to ever disconnect from the network," Brenda added. "That's what we figured out, when all three of us started messing up."

Ava bit her lip.

"But . . . the three of you seem fine now," she said. She tilted her head, peering at her mother. "Did you reprogram everyone?"

"Nothing that permanent," Brenda said. "Or noticeable. I just adapted our settings so we're equally as comfortable with a network of three. Denise, Donald, and I are all linked now. We have full access to each other's thoughts, memories, and knowledge, if we wish."

"It's incredible how strong and clear the link is when it's just the three of us, not the entire robot network," Dad marveled, shaking his head in awe. "It's a more powerful bond. . . . I feel so much smarter now!"

Mom and Brenda beamed at him.

"I never appreciated how much there was to know about building!" Mom said, with more enthusiasm than she'd ever shown for anything that didn't involve five-syllable psychology words. Was this why Mom was suddenly capable of stacking rocks without complaining? Because she was channeling Dad so intensely? "And I'm amazed at what a talented computer programmer Brenda is. I never knew. I could never pick out her individual genius in the midst of all the other computer programmers."

This is a little . . . sick, Eryn thought. *My mother is not only best friends with her husband's ex-wife now, but they kind of . . . share a brain? With my dad, her ex-husband, too?*

"You're being too kind, Denise," Brenda said, shaking back her long, curly red hair. "Of course we'll loop Michael in to our network too, once he's back. And for the first time in your lives, Ava, you and Jackson will be able to take part in a robotic mental link."

Ava's jaw dropped, and her eyes widened.

"You mean . . . ," she began.

"Right," Brenda said, with a broad smile. "We can bring you in, because no one else will ever know. Come here and I'll make the necessary changes." She reached for her daughter. "It will only take a minute and then . . ."

But Ava backed away from Brenda. She smashed against the wall.

"No," Ava whispered. "No, I . . ."

"Ava?" Brenda said uncertainly. "I thought you'd be thrilled."

"You can't do this to me!" Ava screamed. "I won't let you!"

And then she shoved open the door and ran away, out into the shrieking wind.

FOURTEEN

Nick

"Ava!" Brenda screamed, starting to chase after her daughter.

Something made Nick step forward and stop her. Some half-formed thought in his head.

Is it possible that . . .

"Why don't you let me go after her?" he asked. "I know how Mom and Eryn get sometimes, arguing. . . . Ava might listen better to me right now."

"Ava isn't like that," Brenda mumbled. "We don't argue. We . . ."

But she didn't rush for the door again, so Nick took that as permission. He squeezed out the door after Ava.

Eryn came after him.

"Should I come too?" she asked doubtfully, hanging half in and half out of the shed. Eryn wasn't the type to ever be doubtful. Maybe she wasn't falling apart like some malfunctioning robot, but the past few days had taken a toll on her, too.

"We probably shouldn't look like we're ganging up on her," Nick admitted.

He really wanted to add, *So why don't you go deal with Ava, and I'll stay in the nice, warm shed? Where the grown-ups will make all the decisions?*

"I think she likes you better than me anyhow," Eryn said, retreating back into the shed and letting the door shut behind her.

What did I just get myself into? he wondered.

The wind screamed in his ears, and the hood of his coat blew over his face. He tugged it back into place. In just the few moments that Nick had lingered talking to Brenda and Eryn, Ava had gotten halfway down the slope toward the entrance to Mammoth Cave.

At least she's smart enough to head for shelter, instead of running deeper into the woods, Nick thought, starting after her.

"Ava, wait!" he called.

Ava didn't turn around. If anything, she began scrambling down the hill even faster.

Maybe she can't even hear me with all this wind, Nick thought, fighting his way forward. He had to walk sideways to keep from being knocked over. *Well, I'll just wait to talk to her once we're in the cave. It's not like she'll go too far in. She doesn't even have a flashlight. Or a jar of . . . what did she call them? "Bioluminescent cave creatures"?*

Ava reached the entrance to the cave, jumped over the chains strung across it, and disappeared into the darkness. A few moments later Nick reached the chains too. He slowed down and climbed over the chains more carefully. He peered into the darkness ahead.

"Ava?" he called, a little spooked that she was already so far ahead of him that he couldn't see her. Not until his eyes adjusted to the darkness, anyway. "I'm not here to make you go back and do what your mom says. I just want to talk."

Right, because I am so good at talking to girls, Nick thought.

He reminded himself that this wasn't just any girl. Ava was his stepsister. So this was practically like talking to Eryn.

Except that Eryn, as his twin, had been around him since before they were even born.

And Eryn, like him, was human. They understood each other, because they were so much alike.

He sighed.

"Ava, *please*," he called. "Wouldn't you rather talk to me than have the adults come running after you? That's what they're going to do, if we don't go back to the shed soon. Because, you know, they're the most overprotective parents on the planet?"

Ava stepped out of the shadows.

"And I'm one of the most endangered kids on the planet," she said bitterly. "Me and Jackson both. So we get double doses of overprotection."

"That's probably not the right way to look at ... uh ..." Nick stopped, because something hit him. Maybe Ava— and Jackson—didn't even know what had happened to all the *legal* robot children who'd been twelve or under, and what would ultimately happen to all robot kids once Nick and Eryn and the other kids their age grew up. The younger ones had already all been destroyed; the older ones were going to be. Because as Nick and Eryn's generation grew up and then eventually grew old, the goal was for there to ultimately be nothing but humans left.

And that was even if Nick and Eryn *didn't* follow the instructions on the papers he had right now in his upper coat pocket. Every robot in the world was slated for destruction eventually—the paper just urged Nick and Eryn to do that immediately.

It was something Nick himself tried not to think about. And now was really not the time to dwell on it.

"I am *not* letting Mom link me into their little network," Ava said fiercely. Nick was used to Eryn being fierce, but this was scary coming from Ava, with her big eyes and her innocent air. "Would *you* want your parents to have access to every thought you've ever had? To know everything you've ever done? To be able to see, minute by minute, everything you're thinking and doing?"

"*That's* what agreeing to that link would mean?" Nick asked. "No kid would want that! Is your Mom crazy, to think—"

"She's a typical robot," Ava said bitterly. "She doesn't understand."

Nick remembered he was supposed to talk Ava into going back to the shed. Into not hating her mother.

"But isn't there something about how robots can keep some things private?" he asked. "Off-limits to the rest of their network? Isn't that how your mom and dad—and everyone working with them, like my parents—managed to keep you and Jackson secret for the past twelve years?"

"Yeah, but when it's my own parents, do you think they would respect my right to privacy?" Ava asked. It was jarring to hear her soft voice sound so resentful. "When they feel like they *created* Jackson and me, when they *programmed* us, when they see us as their little experiments, to tinker with however they want . . . ?"

In the dim light of the cave, Nick saw Ava's eyes dart to the side, almost as if she was afraid *he* would be able to read her mind too.

And, suddenly, he thought he could.

"You have something you want to keep secret," he said. "Something you really, really, really don't want your parents to know."

The idea that had propelled him out the shed door, to run after Ava, began to take shape in his mind. It had only been half-formed before, but now he was certain it was right. And he was so sick of secrets and suspicions and distrust.

With shaking hands, he pulled the zipper of his coat halfway down so he could reach into the pocket tucked away inside. He pulled out the thick wad of papers, folded in half and then halved again—the papers he'd been carrying around all day, the ones he and Eryn had found in the secret room the night before.

"Is *this* what you don't want your parents to know about?" he asked, holding the papers out to Ava.

FIFTEEN

Ava

"No," Ava whispered. "No. I mean . . . maybe?"

What was she supposed to say? How much did he know?

Nick jerked his hand back, and started stuffing the papers back into his coat.

"Never mind," he said. "I don't know what I was thinking—I thought maybe I'd trick you—I play pranks like that on Eryn all the time. . . . These are nothing. . . . They're all blank. . . ."

Ava saw that he'd left himself an out. That he'd pulled out those terrifying papers thinking he would be able to laugh everything off and pretend he was just playing a prank, if she didn't respond the right way.

If she really didn't know what they were.

"Nick, stop it," Ava said impatiently. "I did see those papers last night before you hid them away—Jackson and I both did. Pretending they don't exist isn't going to help anyone. I know what they say: 'Our own robots were the ones who destroyed us. You must destroy your robots before they destroy you.'"

It was so hard just speaking those words. She mentally checked herself for signs that she might immediately collapse: Light-headedness? Dizziness? Racing pulse?

Oddly, she felt okay. Just a little anxious. But she'd felt that way constantly for the past several months, ever since Dad and Mom explained that she and Jackson had to be homeschooled because it was too dangerous for them be around other kids. Around *normal* kids. Around humans.

Nick pulled the papers back out, unfolded them, looked closely at the top sheet, and then dropped his hand.

"You . . . you *memorized* that?" he asked, his tone wavering between horror and awe.

"I'm a robot," Ava said, the bitterness back in her voice. "Memorizing's easy. It's not like I did it on purpose."

Nick started riffling through the pages.

"Did you memorize all of it?" he asked.

Ava wondered if there was any value in lying. She decided it would take too much effort. And . . . it seemed like he was being honest with her now. So lying to him would be wrong.

"No, so don't start quizzing me or anything," she said. "I only saw the top page before you hid it all. I don't have X-ray vision. Not that X-ray vision would even work— it wouldn't let me see through one page to see what's on the next one down. They almost always depict that wrong in cartoons and superhero movies. . . ."

It was so much easier to babble about X-ray vision and cartoons and superheroes than the fact that the papers Nick was holding told him he was supposed to kill her.

Or just "destroy" me, she corrected herself.

The slightly nicer word didn't help at all.

"Did . . . did any of the grown-ups see these papers?" Nick asked. "Have *all* you robots just been pretending since last night . . . waiting to see what Eryn and I are going to do . . . ?"

"There's no way the grown-ups saw the papers," Ava said, like she was comforting him. "You hid them so fast. And all our parents were *behind* Jackson and me, walking into that room. We're younger and faster and our eyes . . . work a little better."

There. That got the issue of the illegally enhanced vision out of the way without Nick even noticing. He was staring down at the papers in his hands as if they were all that mattered.

"Besides," Ava added, "don't you think that if any of the adults had seen those papers, they would have said something immediately?"

Nick's face relaxed, as if he knew Ava was right.

"Why didn't you tell your parents right away?" Nick asked, glancing back at her. "Why didn't you narc?"

Should Ava bat her eyes and murmur, *Because I knew from the very beginning that you wouldn't actually follow those instructions*? Should she lull him into a false sense of security by emphasizing how much she trusted him and Eryn—when she really didn't? Should she make herself look stronger and more decisive than she really was?

Ava let out a sigh. She swallowed hard.

"The truth?" she said. "Until now, I couldn't even think about those papers without feeling like I was going to fall apart and crash to the ground, just like Jackson. I'm pretty sure that's why *he* blacked out too. So it was like we *couldn't* tell anyone. We wouldn't be able to get the words out without collapsing."

"You're not collapsing now," Nick said. He made it sound like a brilliant observation.

Okay, maybe it is a brilliant observation, Ava thought. *Why* don't *I feel dizzy and queasy and out of control? Those papers are about someone wanting to* kill *me. About my life* ending. *About my own stepbrother and stepsister doing me in.*

She almost giggled at her own brain offering the phrase "doing me in."

Except for that, though, she didn't exactly feel happy thinking those thoughts. She didn't feel like skipping through fields of flowers and gazing at rainbows and wishing for unicorns to come out and play. But she didn't feel like passing out, either.

"I think . . . I think it's because I don't believe anymore that those papers are going to lead to anyone killing me," Ava said slowly. "Maybe it's just because you and Eryn haven't tried to kill me yet, so I don't think you're going to. Maybe I've realized that I could fend you off, if I had to. And I really don't think you're going to show those papers to any . . . hired assassins."

She tried to flash a sarcastic grin at him. It was the kind of thing Eryn was really good at, but Ava's face muscles didn't work the same way. She had a feeling she just looked tentative. Pitiful.

Pitiable.

"Eryn and I agreed last night, we aren't going to follow those instructions," Nick said. "We don't want to destroy anyone. Or anything. But don't you see? If it's true that robots destroyed humanity the last time around, we have to do *something* to make sure it doesn't happen again."

"*I'm* not the type of robot who wants to destroy anyone," Ava said, blinking in a way that she knew made her look sweet and innocent. "I wasn't designed or programmed for that. Can't we work together, to make sure that everyone's safe? Robots *and* humans?"

"Yes," Nick said. "Yes. That's what I want."

Ava felt a pang of guilt. Should she have admitted how much she and Jackson had altered themselves from their original design, their original programming?

Should she have mentioned that she and Jackson didn't always agree?

SIXTEEN

Jackson

Jackson slid into the driver's seat of the van. He started to fasten his seat belt, then changed his mind. First he climbed back to the row of seats where he'd been hiding, picked up the blanket he'd hidden under, folded it into a neat square, and positioned it on the seat cushion beneath the steering wheel. Then he sat down again.

There, he told himself. *Now I look taller.*

Keeping his winter coat on made him look bigger and bulkier. He couldn't make his face look any older right now, but if everything went well, nobody would get close enough to get a good look at his face.

"Okay, Dad," he said aloud. "I hope that HOW TO DRIVE file didn't leave out anything important. I hope you transmitted it all before you collapsed."

He'd carefully laid his dad's body across the seat behind him, where Jackson could keep an eye on him but nobody outside would be able to see him without looking closely.

Dad didn't move. He gave no sign that he'd heard, no sign that he was anything but an inanimate object.

Jackson had never seen any robot shut down so thoroughly. He'd never been to one of the "funerals" that occurred occasionally, the fake proceedings that the robots who ran the world enacted every now and then to get human children used to the notion that death was a part of life. He'd never had a pet—Dad and Mom had always said their family's life was complicated enough already—so he'd never been eased into the notion of death by watching a beloved dog or cat fade away.

On the contrary, Mom and Dad had always acted like they expected Jackson and Ava to be able to live forever. And like Mom and Dad might live forever too.

Dad's not dead, Jackson reminded himself. *This is temporary. He trusts me to get him back to the nature preserve. And then everything will be fine.*

Jackson blinked a couple of times—just to make sure he was seeing straight! Not because any excess moisture might have started pooling in his eyes! Not because he was in any danger of shorting out any circuits! He clicked his seat belt together, pressed his foot on the brake, put his finger on the start button, and shifted into gear.

"See? It's easy," he said out loud. "I know exactly what I'm doing."

He eased his foot off the brake and pressed the accelerator. The van lurched forward, jerked suddenly to a stop, and lurched again.

Okay, that's why there was that bit about applying steady pressure, Jackson thought. *I can do that.*

This time he turned the steering wheel to the right as he pressed his foot down. The van was more responsive than he expected—it shot past the edge of the gravel parking lot and into the grass before Jackson jerked the steering wheel in the other direction. He narrowly missed swinging into the ditch.

Is driving one of those things where you mostly have to learn by doing it, rather than being told about it? he wondered. *Or maybe if I could just tap into the robot network, all that extra knowledge would help me along. . . .*

He didn't think he should try to access the robot network now. He darted a glance back at Dad, flat on the seat. Had Dad shut himself down to *avoid* being linked to the robot network?

Jackson couldn't think about that now. He went back to peering out the windshield and concentrating on making his driving steadier and less jerky. It would probably be good if he could get the hang of steering now, before he got out on the road. In the parking lot it was okay to drive at a speed he himself could outrun, but he couldn't creep along at five miles per hour all the way back to the nature preserve. He was just glad there didn't seem to be anyone out and about to watch him. At least not anyone he could see.

Surely this is such a small town I'll be out of it in no time at all, he told himself. *It's windy and cold—it's not like anybody's going to be sitting out on their porches waving at whoever goes by. And then the highway's likely to be totally deserted, all the way back to the nature preserve. . . . This isn't that hard.*

Jackson inched out of the parking lot. To his relief, he could remember the way back to the nature preserve— the pattern of turns and the distances in between—from before, when Dad was driving, while Jackson was huddled under the blanket. The route wasn't complicated, and after a few blocks of crawling along, he saw signs that said TO I-65. A few more turns and he faced the entrance ramp to the freeway.

You'll really have to go fast now, he told himself. *There's a minimum speed on the highway—you could be stopped by the cops if you're going too slow. . . .*

The traffic signal ahead of him changed, and he hit the accelerator. It felt like he was going a million miles an hour. The wind slammed against the side of the van—maybe he would even tip over.

But when he dropped his gaze to the speedometer for an instant, he saw that he was only going thirty-five.

Faster, faster, faster, he told himself, squealing his tires as he swerved from the ramp onto the highway itself. It was good there was no other traffic, because he slipped back and forth between the right and left lanes before he managed to pull the van onto a reasonably straight path.

No way you're going to tip over, he tried to comfort himself. *This van probably weighs a couple tons. The wind would have to hit it at an incredible speed to actually flip the van. Maybe . . . let's see . . . carry the one . . . two hundred miles an hour?*

The wind could not possibly be going two hundred miles an hour. Although it *was* strangely strong. Surely Jackson could do a better job of controlling the van if there weren't so much wind.

Just another twenty-five minutes of this, he told himself. *It's a straight shot. No surprises.*

That was when he saw the black-and-gold car parked in the median.

Is that . . . highway patrol? he thought, his heart beating faster. Or, well, what substituted for his heart.

No need to panic, he told himself. *Unless the cops get a good look at my face, there's no reason for them to suspect I'm driving without a license. There's no reason for them to stop me and check. I'm not doing anything wrong—except that thing about driving without a license. . . .*

Jackson's enhanced vision meant that he noticed the partially hidden highway patrol car a full five minutes before he was going to pass it. Jackson spent those five minutes telling himself, *Don't do anything wrong. Don't do anything wrong. Don't do anything wrong. . . .* He gripped the steering wheel so tightly his knuckles ached. He didn't let the wheels of the van deviate at all from their straight path ahead.

Just as he closed in on the spot where the highway patrol car was hidden, Jackson turned his head to the right, as if to check his side-view mirror or glance at trees bending in the wind. Actually, he was making sure the cops wouldn't see his too-young face. But it threw him a little off-balance, and the highway jogged ever so slightly to the left just past the cop car. So he couldn't just keep going straight. He had to turn a little.

Not too much, not too much, he told himself. He went too far, and the van started to veer into the other lane. He jerked the steering wheel back to the right, but he overcorrected. One tire hit the line of bumps at the side of the highway, and the grating sound seemed loud enough to wake the dead—or at least Jackson's father.

No, no, no, Jackson thought.

He managed to hold on to the steering wheel. The highway went back to being totally straight, nothing but one continuous hundred-eighty-degree angle.

That wasn't so bad, Jackson thought. *The cops probably didn't even notice. . . .*

He dared to glance at the rearview mirror. The highway patrol car had its turn signal on. It pulled out onto the highway, into the lane right behind Jackson.

Yes, but it doesn't have a siren or lights on, Jackson told himself. *It's just a coincidence that it's driving behind me. . . .*

Jackson didn't think it was a coincidence.

He slowed down a little. Maybe the cop car would pass him.

It didn't.

Jackson sped up, until he was going an entire mile per hour over the speed limit.

The cop car sped up too.

Okay, just don't make any mistakes, he told himself.

He started sweating, and his ears rang the way they sometimes did right before he blacked out.

Can't do that, he told himself. No shorting out. Not now.

Ahead of him there was a little hill. The cop car followed Jackson at a very precise distance of six car lengths. That meant that once Jackson's van crested the hill, he would have at least a moment or two when the cops couldn't see him.

Could I pull into the woods then? Jackson wondered. *Could I hide the van completely in just that amount of time, if I were going fast enough?*

No, he'd crash into the trees, and the cops would stop and ask for his license for sure.

That is, if Jackson even survived the crash.

Fat globules of sweat ran down his face and into his eyes. He flicked them away, making the van swerve again. In the rearview mirror, he saw the cop in the driver's seat lift her arm a little uncertainly, as if she was thinking about pulling him over but hadn't quite decided yet. The cop sitting beside her said something, but Jackson couldn't let himself watch long enough to read lips.

He could not keep driving in front of these cops. He was bound to make some mistake that would make them too suspicious not to stop him. After all, he had only fifteen minutes of driving experience—how could he *not* make mistakes?

He reached the top of the hill and immediately began peering around at everything on the downhill slope. Just past the hill's crest, a gravel lane connected his side of the highway with the lanes going the opposite way. There wasn't even time to calculate if it was safe—or possible—but he swung his wheel as sharply as he could to the left, aiming for that lane.

The van shivered and shook. One side of his tires missed the gravel lane entirely and smashed into the grass. Jackson swerved, struggling to hang on to the steering wheel. He jerked it even more to the left and slammed his foot on the brake.

Even with Jackson's robotically precise sense of time, it felt like an eternity passed before the van came to a jerky stop. He was half on and half off the berm of the other side of the highway, facing perpendicular to the road. A wide trench of exposed dirt lay behind him where his tires had torn up the grass.

Before he even took time for a deep breath, Jackson

made himself look for the cop car. It was past the gravel lane connecting the two sides of the highway, and there was no way the cop car would drive over the grass and risk tearing up even more.

They're robots, Jackson told himself. *They won't violate a rule like that.*

Based on how evenly spaced the gravel connectors had been elsewhere along the highway, the next closest one was probably five miles away. So Jackson probably had at least four or five minutes before the cops returned to interrogate him—and undoubtedly arrest him too.

That is, unless there was *another* cop car close by that the first cops could send after him. He couldn't count on having much time at all.

Shaking, Jackson looked both ways for traffic—there was nothing coming, in either direction—and then he drove on across the lanes ahead of him. He came to an abrupt stop in the ditch on the opposite side of the highway.

"Okay, Dad, why didn't you also download instructions into my brain for BEST WAYS TO CARRY AN UNCONSCIOUS MAN?" he muttered.

He undid his seat belt and slid out of his seat—which was hard to do when his legs were shaking every bit as hard as the rest of his body. He bent over Dad and pulled his father's body toward the van's sliding door. He opened it and jumped out.

And then he wrapped the shopping bag full of electronic supplies around one of his wrists, eased his father's body out of the van, and half carried, half dragged Dad toward the woods.

Not the woods closest to the van. He aimed for the ones that he could reach only by crossing four lanes of highway and a grassy median and another ditch—the woods on the completely opposite side of the road.

SEVENTEEN

Nick

Eryn is going to be so mad at me, Nick thought, even as he peered at Ava's soft smile and the glow of relief in her eyes over the partnership they'd just formed.

He didn't think Eryn would automatically oppose working with Ava—or Jackson, for that matter. Not exactly. It was just that Eryn always made such a big deal about how closely she and Nick were linked, how they had that twin bond that meant they could practically read each other's minds.

They *were* pretty good at finishing each other's sentences.

So when it came to something like keeping the papers secret—which was, oh, only the biggest dilemma the two of them had ever faced—he knew she would have liked to be consulted.

Actually, what she usually likes is to make up her

own mind and then have me agree that she's right, Nick thought with a sigh.

He imagined telling Eryn, *Hey, I had to make a snap decision and you weren't there! There wasn't time to consult you!* You *were the one who said it was best for me to go after Ava by myself!*

Nope, wouldn't work. None of that would keep her from being mad.

Ava's smile turned a little tentative. Maybe she was responding to his sigh. Or the grimace that had started spreading over his face.

"So, want to go back to that shed, before the parents come after us?" she asked, sounding as if that was the last thing she wanted.

"It would be a good strategy," Nick said with an apologetic shrug. "Gives you an edge, that you're returning *voluntarily.*"

Usually it was Eryn who thought more about ways to outsmart their parents. He felt a little bit like he was channeling her ideas.

Which made him feel even more disloyal.

"I guess," Ava said, with a helpless shrug. "Got any ideas for how I can keep from joining their network when we go back? About what excuse I can use?"

"You *can't* mention the papers," Nick said, panic rising inside him. He really didn't want to have Eryn mad at him *plus* Mom, Dad, and probably even Brenda. And Michael, when he got back.

The adults *would* be mad, wouldn't they?

"Of course I won't say anything about the papers," Ava said, sounding offended that he'd suggest such a thing. "I need something that sounds calm and rational, and makes them feel calm and rational, too. . . ."

Nick snapped his fingers.

"I've got it!" he said. "Listen, just let me do the talking—you'll be fine."

Eryn would have insisted on knowing his plan, but Ava nodded trustingly.

"Okay," she said, shrugging again. "Let's go."

They trudged back uphill toward the shed. Nick couldn't understand—he'd felt like he was struggling against the wind the whole way down to the cave, and now that he was going back up he *still* felt like it was pushing him backward.

That did not mean that he couldn't win, no matter what he did. It couldn't.

It just means . . . Lida Mae was right, he thought. *There is an awful storm blowing in.*

They shoved their way back into the shed.

"Ava—" Brenda began.

Nick held up his hand to stop her.

"Please," he said. "Let me explain for Ava. I told her I could do it calmly and rationally, and you would all understand."

That would help, wouldn't it? To appeal to the adults' sense that they were all so compassionate and understanding? The perfect parents they were programmed to be?

He turned to his own mother.

"Mom, you're a middle school psychologist," he said. "This should be easy for you. Think about everything you know about the mind of a typical adolescent human." He flicked his gaze toward Brenda and Dad, too. "I don't really understand how this works, but I guess the two of you can 'remember' everything Mom knows about adolescent psychology too. You're entirely clued in."

"Yes, that's true," Brenda started to say. "But that doesn't matter, because Ava isn't a—"

Nick made the *stop!* signal with his hand again.

"Think about it," he said. "You guys *designed* Ava to fool people into thinking she's human. And now you're upset with her because you succeeded too well? Ava is a robot, yes, but she's not the same kind of robot as you adults. Even though she's not human, she's more *like* a real human than you all are—a real human *kid*. She wants independence and privacy and . . . and self-actualization, just like any other twelve-year-old."

Nick was really proud of himself for pulling out that term, "self-actualization." He wasn't entirely sure what it meant, but Mom talked about it all the time. He figured it had to be important.

Eryn grinned at him, as if she thoroughly enjoyed his performance. It made Nick feel a little guilty again, and he forgot what he'd planned to say next.

"And, uh, you don't want to hurt Ava's, uh . . . ," he tried, hoping the thought would come back to him soon.

"Oh, I see," Mom said, nodding slowly. "Are you saying that the very idea of joining a robot network created such a strong cognitive dissonance for Ava that she descended into the tumultuous, tempestuous behavior of a typical adolescent human female?"

Nick was pretty good at imitating Mom sometimes, but there was no way that crazy sentence would have come out of *his* mouth.

Eryn's eyes danced.

"I think that *was* what he was about to say," she

agreed. She was standing behind the grown-ups, so she risked giving Nick a private smirk before grabbing Mom's shoulder and telling her, "Mom! I'm surprised at you! Why didn't you figure out Ava would get, uh, cognitive dissonance?"

Oh, yeah, Nick thought, his stomach giving a guilty twist. *Eryn's loving this.*

Would that make things better or worse when she found out what Nick and Ava had really talked about in the cave?

"Oh, Ava, please stop looking so apologetic," Brenda burst out. Nick realized that the whole time he'd been talking, Ava had kept her eyes downcast, demurely peering at the ground. "We get it! We understand! This isn't your fault! We were wrong even to think about looping you in to the robot network."

Ava looked up.

"Thank you," she whispered, tears glistening in her eyes.

Nick was pretty sure they were supposed to indicate joy or relief, not sorrow.

Thank you, Ava mouthed again, facing him.

Crisis over, Nick thought. *Or at least one of them. I wish I knew how to solve all the others. . . .*

Just then there was thumping at the door behind Nick. Brenda flew toward the door before he could react.

"Jackson? Michael?" she called hopefully.

"Sorry, no. It's me again," a girl's voice responded, even as the door creaked back, and Lida Mae poked her freckled face into the narrow opening.

Oh no. Oh no, Nick thought, exchanging horrified glances with first Eryn, than Ava. How much of that conversation had Lida Mae heard? Had she heard Brenda say "robot network"?

Had she heard Nick say, "Ava is a robot, yes, but she's not the same kind of robot as all of you?"

EIGHTEEN

Eryn

Was it possible to get emotional whiplash?

If so, Eryn had it.

First she'd had to hold in laughter over how Nick totally took down the grown-ups, using some of Mom's own crazy psychology terms. Personally, Eryn had no idea why Ava cared so much about the stupid robot network. (Unless . . . was Nick maybe telling the truth? Was Ava that much like a human kid, that she didn't want her parents to know what she was thinking?)

Then Eryn got kind of mad at Ava. Why was she letting Nick do all the talking? Why did she just stare at the ground, as meek as could be, instead of standing up for herself?

If Ava wants to fool people into thinking she's actually human, she's got to do better than that, Eryn thought. *Grow a spine! Or . . . at least . . . have one implanted.*

Then suddenly Lida Mae was there, and Eryn had to worry about what she'd heard.

If Lida Mae really had heard them talking about robots—if she even knew what robots were—wouldn't she mention it right away?

Lida Mae's eyes darted about anxiously. But when she spoke, all she said was "The storm's starting up faster than I expected. You'uns need to head into the cave now."

Eryn let out a silent sigh of relief. But she saw identical worried expressions settle on all the adults' faces.

"We can't go anywhere until my husband and stepson get back," Mom said. "They won't know where to find us."

"Leave a note," Lida Mae said. "If your husband knows anything about surviving in the wilderness, he'll know to shelter in place, and he won't come looking for you until after the storm."

Nobody answered her. Lida Mae turned her head side to side, her eyes narrowed.

"Your husband and stepson—they do know *something* about surviving in the wilderness, don't they?" she asked.

Michael and Jackson are robots, Eryn reminded herself. *I bet they're not in danger from a blizzard anyhow. Everybody's just acting like they are so Lida Mae doesn't get suspicious.*

But even she didn't feel like this was true. And she really didn't know—could robots be ruined in a storm?

Blindly, Eryn snatched up one of the backpacks leaning against the shed wall.

"I'm sure Michael and Jackson will be fine," she said. It felt like a lie. It felt like anyone could have told she was lying. She soldiered on anyhow. "But, Lida Mae, I'm glad you're watching out for the rest of us."

"Er . . . right," Nick said, following her lead and grabbing his backpack just as blindly. "Thanks, Lida Mae."

Their movement seemed to wake up everyone else, and a few moments later all of them—three kids, three adults—began following Lida Mae downhill toward the cave's mouth. The wind was ferocious now, and by the time Eryn reached the bottom of the hill, its gusts contained ice pellets that stung her cheeks.

"Into the cave, into the cave—quick!" Lida Mae shouted, holding out a hand to help them over the chains at the cave's entrance. "Then if you keep going straight you'll hit the Rotunda, the big open space where you can wait out the storm. . . ."

Eryn, Nick, and Ava stepped over the chains and past the array of KEEP OUT signs. Dad, Mom, and Brenda stopped on the other side of the chains.

"Young lady, you were right!" Dad told Lida Mae as he shook his wild hair back out of his face. Ice pellets glistened in his curls, and his face was red with the cold. "This is awful! I have to insist: Unless you're going to ride out the storm with us, you should go back to your family immediately! Before this gets any worse!"

"And maybe some of us should go with you?" Brenda suggested tentatively. "Just to make sure you're safe?"

Lida Mae's face tightened.

"Oh no, I'll be fine," she said. Her expression broke into a mischievous grin. Eryn wondered if it was fake. "Actually, I'm just going to cut through the cave. That way I can come back and forth to check on you."

Nick jabbed Eryn in the ribs.

"What if her family lives *in* the cave?" he whispered. "Or right on top of one of the other entrances?"

"It's possible," Eryn admitted. This could have been a good clue, but she didn't have time to think about it right now. Not when Mom, Dad, and Brenda were still standing so awkwardly on the other side of the chains.

Won't Lida Mae wonder why they won't step past the KEEP OUT *signs?* Eryn wondered. *What if they absolutely can't?*

Robots were such rule-followers. The adults had said

the night before that Ava and Jackson could easily disobey the warnings, because they hadn't been designed to think of themselves as robots. But the adults could disobey KEEP OUT signs only if it was their parental duty—only if they needed to protect or rescue their kids.

Eryn took a few steps deeper into the cave. Into the darkness.

"Look, Mom, Dad, Brenda—I'm getting into a dangerous situation," she called back over her shoulder. "What if there's a rockslide or a sinkhole, and you're not here to protect me?"

She tried to make her voice light and teasing, so Lida Mae would think she was just joking around. But robots weren't always great at detecting humor. So maybe her words alone would enable Mom and Dad to defy the signs and cross the chains and come after her.

"You can't scare us," Brenda muttered. "Not after we heard Lida Mae say she'd keep you in safe places."

"And not when all the evidence we can gather would seem to indicate she's right," Mom agreed.

Their words should have sounded cheerful—surely they were glad Lida Mae was going to keep their kids safe. But their tones were glum.

Would Lida Mae notice?

"But . . . the three of you can't just stand there," Ava said, her voice ringing with dismay. "You'll freeze!"

Was Ava trying to trigger some self-preservation response in the adults? Was that another rule robots might have to follow, one that could overrule the need to obey KEEP OUT signs?

Eryn whipped her head back to check the adults' reaction.

They looked grimmer than ever. Then, suddenly, all three of their expressions brightened.

"Of course we're not just going to stand here," Dad announced, squaring his shoulders. "We're going back to . . ."

"Rescue Michael and Jackson," Mom finished.

NINETEEN

Ava

"That's not safe!" Lida Mae cried. The words were ripped from her mouth by the wailing wind. "It doesn't make any sense! What are you talking about? You're the adults—you're supposed to be the sensible ones!"

Ava saw all three adults grit their teeth simultaneously. Maybe the makeshift robot network Mom had built made them a little too similar.

They need to be careful, Ava thought. *What can I do to distract Lida Mae?*

"Actually," Ava said, trying for her sweetest, most innocent, most persuasive voice, "they're just being responsible, Lida Mae. I know you're trying to take good care of all of us, but the adults really are better in the wilderness than you think. Come on. Let's get to the safe place in the cave, and the adults can join us later."

She grabbed Lida Mae's arm and tugged. Maybe Ava's parents should have designed Ava with a little more strength—or maybe Ava herself should have added that—because Lida Mae shrugged off Ava's hand and ignored her.

"This is pure dad-blame craziness!" Lida Mae exclaimed. "You're proving you don't understand wilderness conditions, just by saying you plan to go traipsing out into a blizzard. People get lost in these conditions if they don't take shelter! People die!"

"Mom, Dad—you will be safe, won't you?" Eryn practically whimpered.

She doesn't actually know, Ava realized. *Nick and Eryn aren't sure how much cold and ice robots can withstand.*

"Tell Eryn they can survive better in a blizzard than the two of you," Ava whispered in Nick's ear. He was standing closer, and Ava didn't think she could say something directly to Eryn without Lida Mae hearing her too.

"Don't worry," Ava's stepmother, Denise, said calmly. "We'll take every precaution."

The other two adults nodded beside her, just as calmly.

"If you were taking every precaution, you'd come on into the cave with your kids!" Lida Mae protested. "*That's* 'taking every precaution'!"

"Here," Donald said, handing flashlights across the chains to Ava and Nick. "This way you kids have two of the lights and we'll have two. For later. When we come back to the cave with Jackson and Michael."

He might as well have added a *wink-wink-nod-nod* gesture. Ava knew he was trying to tell her and his own kids, *You know none of us adults can go past these signs unless we think you're in danger. Which you're not. But we have to pretend we can, so Lida Mae doesn't get suspicious. That's why we can't give you all the flashlights.*

"No!" Lida Mae shouted. "I insist! Come into the cave now!"

She grabbed for Donald's arm, but he jerked it away. The motion pulled Lida Mae toward the chains, and she fell over them.

"Sorry," Donald mumbled, backing away even more. "But we've got to go. Now. Before the snow gets worse. Kids, be careful. And stay in the cave."

All three adults spun around and began scrambling up the hill again.

Ava and Nick tried to help Lida Mae up, but she seemed fighting mad. She kept shaking their hands off, shoving them away.

"Let go!" she screamed at Ava and Nick.

"Come back!" she screamed at the adults.

The adults didn't stop. They started running instead, getting farther and farther away. Lida Mae hurdled the chains and took off after them.

"Mom? Dad? Brenda? Lida Mae? Wait!" Eryn screamed from behind Ava. "Let us come too! Don't leave us behind!"

Ava grabbed Eryn's arm before Eryn could leap over the chains. Maybe Ava had gotten stronger in the past two minutes; maybe Eryn just wasn't as determined or forceful as Lida Mae. Even though Eryn tried to pull away, Ava held firm.

For good measure, Ava reached out and grabbed Nick's arm too.

"*Think*," she whispered to the other two kids. "You two really would be in danger of dying out there. The adults will be fine. They'll just find somewhere to hide from Lida Mae. And Lida Mae can take care of herself."

Eryn jerked back, and this time Ava let go.

"I . . . I wasn't really scared," Eryn said stiffly. "I was trying to trigger that—what's it called? The parental imperative?—in Mom and Dad. So maybe they would be able to come into the cave with us, if they thought it was the only alternative to us wandering around in some blizzard with them."

Ava thought maybe Eryn was lying. Or exaggerating, anyway. She really did look scared, with her lips pressed tightly together and her eyebrows furrowed with worry.

Up the hill, the adults and Lida Mae disappeared into the swirling whiteness.

"Are you sure our parents are all right out there?" Nick asked plaintively. "And Michael and Jackson, too, I guess . . . Can robots withstand extreme cold and snow and ice? Can they survive a blizzard?"

"Of course they can," Ava said, her voice coming out strong and confident. "No problem. Remember how all the embryos that were used to restart the human race were frozen for centuries? Didn't you think about how there were robots taking care of them? So robots are great with cold temperatures. And ice and snow."

And . . . now I'm lying, Ava thought, amazed at herself. *Or at least passing off false logic as truth.*

There was a difference between robots temporarily dealing with frozen embryos and robots running through a blizzard for a long period of time. Yes, robots could withstand bad weather better than humans could, but they could break down in extreme cold. Their circuitry and memory cards could be destroyed by long exposure to ice and snow.

But if I tell Eryn and Nick that, they really will go running out into the snow after their parents, Ava thought. *They're humans. Ruled by emotion, not logic. I have to lie to save them.*

Was that why the lie flowed off her tongue so easily? Almost as if it had been . . . programmed?

Do I have programming I never discovered before? Ava wondered. *Just because I've never been in a situation before where I could influence anyone making a life-or-death decision? Did Dad—and Mom—design Jackson and me to have the same obligation to save humans that they themselves have? To value human needs and lives above our own?*

If that was the case, why wasn't Ava worried about Lida Mae?

While Ava was standing there trying to figure her own self out, Eryn and Nick were both leaning out over the chains, as if still trying to catch a glimpse of the adults and Lida Mae out in the snow beyond.

Ava pulled them both back.

"Come on," she said. "You're going to get frostbite standing there. Let's go to that Rotunda that Lida Mae was talking about."

Eryn frowned. Nick stomped his feet.

But they both still followed Ava deeper into the cave.

TWENTY

Jackson

Dragging his father's body, Jackson reached the edge of the woods with one ear cocked to listen for the sound of a police car behind him.

Not yet, not yet . . .

His progress across the highway and the grassy dividing strip and ditch had been slower than he'd wanted, because he'd paused a few times to make sure he wasn't leaving footprints or drag marks on the ground. He was just lucky the ground was so frozen and the wind was so brisk, erasing his tracks.

So as long as I didn't miscalculate . . .

Miles down the road, he heard a vehicle slow down, maneuver its tires from blacktop onto gravel, and then speed back toward him and Dad.

Okay, so they've turned around, and now they'll see my van off the other side of the road in . . . oh, just under 10.235 seconds, Jackson told himself. *But they won't be able to see me once I step past this next tree.*

Jackson forced himself to take six more steps, dodging six more trees. Then he risked a slight pause, leaning his father's body against a stump for a moment. He surveyed the path he'd just taken, and brushed aside a few broken twigs that might have given them away. He settled the dead leaves he'd disturbed back into place.

"There," Jackson muttered, as if his dad could hear him. "All better."

He estimated that the cops would spend at least an hour searching the other side of the highway before they realized he could have scrambled over to a more distant hiding place—an action that would defy all robot logic.

Did that mean he had time to reboot his father? And then let Dad rewire Jackson's innards too?

Jackson went back to listening intently, even as he lifted Dad again and started tugging him toward a small clearing in the woods ahead. Once he determined it was safe, he and Dad would need space to work. Jackson tuned out the wind whipping around him and shrieking through the branches overhead. Behind all that, he could hear car doors slamming. Someone let out a whistle.

"See how that thing's parked?" a woman's voice asked.

"Did you see how he whipped around that corner?" a man replied.

It slowed him down, but Jackson risked glancing back toward the road again. He could see nothing behind him now but dense woods; even leafless, the trees blocked out any glimpse of the highway or the cops' car. That meant the cops' words came through so clearly because of Jackson's extraordinary hearing—not because they were close enough to see him. Jackson estimated they were 0.6382 miles away. Give or take.

"Are you thinking what I'm thinking?" the female cop asked.

"Juvenile," the male replied. "And I mean, a *young* juvenile. Twelve or under."

"So . . . human," the woman agreed. "No robot—not even a teenaged robot—would drive like that."

Shows how much you two know, Jackson thought. *I am capable of driving every bit as recklessly as a human!*

But it worried him that they had concluded he was an illegal driver—and a kid—so quickly. He tried to lift Dad higher and take bigger steps. The wind blew dead leaves around behind them.

"This means all bets are off, figuring out where to

look for this juvenile delinquent," the male cop said. "This fugitive from the law."

"Exactly," the female cop said. "Anyone who drives like that—well, you can't expect him to make *any* logical decisions."

Oh, crap, Jackson thought, picking up his pace even more. *They figured that out way too fast.*

He didn't have time to stop and reboot Dad. He didn't have time to fix his own circuitry, no matter how frayed his wires were. And he *really* didn't have time to break down.

No, no, not going to do that, Jackson assured himself. *You're fine. Dad's counting on you. . . .*

Maybe it would help to forget about the cops and just concentrate on walking? Dragging Dad meant Jackson had to go backward, his head turned awkwardly to watch where he was going. One foot back. Then the other. Then the first foot again . . .

Dad's head thudded against Jackson's chest. Jackson struggled to pull his father's body over a downed log. But his muscles already ached, and by his estimation the campsite was still more than ten miles away. That was if he dared to go straight to the campsite, rather than taking a roundabout way to throw the cops off his trail.

I should have given myself superhuman strength and running skills when I had the chance, Jackson thought. He and Ava had never upgraded their athletic skills. It had always seemed like physical changes would be too hard to hide. But Jackson regretted that now.

"Don't worry, Dad," Jackson whispered. "I'm strong enough. I'm fast enough too. I'm going to make it back to the campsite before those cops find me. No problem. Don't worry. I've got this covered. . . . I do. . . ."

Jackson's head swam. He heard a rustling off in the distance that had to be a twig snapping under the weight of somebody's foot.

Just an animal, he told himself. *Just a squirrel or a chipmunk or . . .*

He couldn't help himself. He turned and looked back toward the highway.

See? No one's there, he told himself. *You might be hearing a mouse in someone's house back in that town you left fifteen minutes ago. . . . You might be hearing a snowflake falling a mile away. . . .*

That was the disadvantage of enhanced hearing. Sometimes it was hard to figure out what was important and what wasn't, when he heard *everything*.

Out of the cacophony of little sounds he heard the

crackle of a police radio, and then the female cop's voice: "Requesting backup . . ."

Jackson shifted his father's weight and started trying to run. But his gait was awkward with his arms around his father's chest, his father's legs dragging. What was more important: going fast, or not leaving a noticeable trail? Dad's torso slipped to the side, and Jackson tilted the other way to keep Dad from falling to the ground. Now he was running backward and sideways, his neck bent, his hands clutching Dad's armpits. The bag of electronic supplies thudded against his leg, an echo to Dad's feet jolting against the ground.

And then Jackson tripped.

No, no, his brain screamed as he fell. *There's no time for this! Not when there are going to be swarms of cops looking for me . . .*

Desperately, he tried to ease his fall, simultaneously going down on one knee, jerking Dad's body higher, and twisting even more to the side so that Dad at least wouldn't hit the ground with full force. But that meant that the weight of Dad's body landed on Jackson.

So what? Jackson told himself. *Just get back up. Just keep running. Just . . .*

Jackson looked down and saw a wire poking out of his torso.

Can't be anything too important if I'm still conscious, he thought. *Splice it back together and go on!*

He tried to reach for the wire, but he couldn't move his arms. The right one was pinned under his body, but the left one was still around Dad's waist. It should have been free and clear and available. Unlike most of the rest of Jackson's body, it didn't even hurt.

It just wouldn't move. It was like it had become an inanimate object, not even connected to Jackson's nervous system.

Is that maybe what that broken wire is about? Jackson thought. *Oh no—what if I'm completely paralyzed? What if I can't move at all, can't do anything to hide from the cops who are looking for me? What if . . . what if . . . what if . . .*

Jackson stopped being able to hear. He stopped being able to see. He stopped being able to think.

And then he felt the internal whirring and zapping that could mean only one thing: His system was completely shutting down.

TWENTY-ONE

Nick

We messed up, Nick thought. *I messed up.*

Even as he walked deeper and deeper into the cave alongside Ava and Eryn, his mind scolded him: *Why didn't you and the girls grab Mom and Dad and Brenda and force them to come into the cave with you? And Lida Mae, too? How could you have let them all run out into the blizzard like that? Why didn't you keep them safe? Why don't you turn around and chase after them now—why don't you rescue them?*

Each time he thought that, he countered himself: *Because Ava said they're fine out there in the cold. They're not in any danger, like we would be. Lida Mae can take care of herself in the wilderness. And all the adults—they're robots.*

But they were also his parents.

Nick had never felt like this before. Until the first day he'd met his stepsiblings—and found out they were robots, setting off the cascade of other revelations—he'd had a pretty simple life. His biggest dilemmas had been things like *How can I talk Mom or Dad into buying me a new lacrosse stick when they know I broke my old one goofing off and not listening to the coach?* And *Do I dare sneak in extra video game time when Mom thinks I'm doing homework?* There had been the whole weirdness of Mom remarrying, but if the adults hadn't been so secretive about Ava and Jackson, Nick would have just adjusted and gotten over it.

For the first twelve years of his life, he'd never had to be anything but a normal, relatively obedient, relatively carefree kid.

But now . . .

Is it possible to break your own brain in half, second-guessing a decision you just made five minutes ago? A decision you could unmake at any moment?

He thought about pulling Eryn aside—out of Ava's earshot—and asking if she thought they should turn around. But he still hadn't told her that Ava knew about the papers rustling in his coat pocket, so he felt weird even looking at Eryn right now.

And, oh no—what are we going to do about these papers? Nick wondered. *Should we have just told the grown-ups about them to begin with, and let them figure things out? Should we go back and do that now? Or as soon as the blizzard's over?*

That is, if the grown-ups survived the blizzard . . .

"Do you mind?" Eryn said.

Nick realized she was talking to him.

"Huh?" he said.

"The flashlight," Eryn said. "The way you're making it bounce all around . . . I can't see where I'm going. Can't you hold it steady? Or . . . let me hold it?"

Nick had kind of forgotten he was holding a flashlight. He'd forgotten Eryn didn't have one. He'd forgotten everything but the questions in his own mind.

"We're walking on a flat trail," Nick said. His voice came out sounding surly. "In a dark cave. There's nothing *to* see."

How could his sister whine about what she could or couldn't see at a time like this?

Eryn cleared her throat, which was always a sign that she was annoyed.

"That's easy for you to say, when you're holding the flashlight," she said. "When you can see there aren't any rocks to trip over in front of *your* feet."

"Here, Eryn," Ava said in a gentle tone. She shifted

her flashlight so the beam illuminated more of the path ahead of Eryn. "Why don't you walk between Nick and me? We'll let the beams overlap, and then you can see."

Eryn snorted—the kind of snort that said, *Stop treating me like a little kid! Stop talking to me like I'm a cranky five-year-old!* But she moved so the three of them could walk shoulder to shoulder, lined up.

They'd taken only three or four more steps when Eryn burst out, "This isn't working! Nick's still making the light bounce, and—"

"I am not!" Nick protested.

"You don't know what it's like not having a flashlight in here!" Eryn said. "Not having any control, and having the darkness press in on you, and not knowing what's happening to Mom and Dad out there . . ."

Okay, it's not really the flashlight making Eryn crazy, Nick thought. *She's freaking out about the same things I'm freaking out about.*

He was about to say, *That's it. Let's turn around,* but Ava spoke first.

"Here," she said, shoving her flashlight into Eryn's hand, making the beam arc wildly. "We'll take turns. I—" Ava stopped walking. She grabbed the flashlight back from Eryn and yanked it upward so the beam stretched toward a point on the wall far, far ahead. It was a spot she'd briefly illuminated a moment before, but this time Ava held the flashlight steady. "What's that?"

"What's what?" Nick asked. As far as he could tell, she was peering at the same kind of endless rock they'd been passing all along.

"On that door . . . ," Ava muttered.

She took off running. Nick and Eryn exchanged glances, then ran after her. Nick didn't even try to keep the flashlight steady, but Eryn didn't complain now.

They caught up with Ava as she approached what did indeed seem to be a door.

"Ava, chill," Nick said, trying not to pant. "It's just the door to the room we were in last night, the room where, uh . . ."

"Yeah, see?" Eryn said, tugging on Nick's arm so his flashlight beam illuminated the doorknob. "Remember the room with the broken desk, and nothing else to see? No need to go in there again, right?"

Ava glanced back over her shoulder.

"Eryn, I know about the papers you and Nick found in that room," she said. "Jackson and I saw Nick hide them. We know what they say."

Nick was stunned that she could say this so flatly, as if it didn't even matter anymore.

Kind of nice of you to let me off the hook, though, he thought. *Now I never have to tell Eryn I showed you the papers without asking her opinion first.*

But Ava had stopped looking at either of them.

"This is *not* the door to the secret room we were in last night," she said. "We passed that on the other side of the hallway a long time ago. And that door had a sign on it about how no robots were allowed in; it was for humans only. This one . . . this . . ."

She started walking again, closer and closer to the door. Nick and Eryn crept behind her. After they'd taken about ten more steps, Ava reached back and put her hand on Nick's flashlight, redirecting it. Now both flashlight beams were aimed toward the top part of the door, where Nick could just barely make out letters and words.

The sign on this door said: FOR ROBOT ACCESS ONLY.

TWENTY-TWO

Eryn

Ava reached for the doorknob.

"No, don't!" Eryn cried, pulling back on her stepsister's arm. "You don't know what's in there!"

"And this is how I'm going to find out," Ava said.

Eryn practically despised Ava for how calm she sounded, how robotically rational. It was almost *evil* that Ava could stay so unaffected, while Eryn's mind raced and her stomach churned and she could just feel her adrenaline levels spiking, as if her body thought she might need to run a marathon sometime in the next few seconds.

"What if it's a trick?" Nick asked. "Or a trap?"

Ava barely paused. "It's not like that other room, where humans could be sure that if they labeled the door ROBOTS NOT ALLOWED PAST THIS POINT, robots would have to obey in almost every circumstance," she said. "Humans can disobey this sign anytime they want. They have free will."

"That's why I think it could be a trap," Nick said. "Because robots know that about humans."

"Sometimes STAY OUT! signs make us want to go into a place even more," Eryn added.

"True," Ava said. "But I really *am* a robot. So I'm not worried." She reached for the doorknob again, muttering to herself, "All these years thinking I was the same as a human . . . It's different now that I know I'm not."

Eryn didn't reach out to stop Ava this time. Neither did Nick.

Ava turned the knob, and the door creaked open. Nick kicked at it as if he didn't have the patience to wait for it to swing open on its own. The motion must have tripped some kind of sensor, because suddenly bright, beautiful light shone out of the room.

"Light," Eryn sighed, even as Nick cried, "Look for booby traps before anyone goes in!"

"It's fine," Ava said. "It's an empty room."

She stepped across the threshold. Eryn and Nick, less bold, just leaned their heads forward, looking in.

It took Eryn a moment for her eyes to adjust, but then she could tell: This room was practically the twin of the room where they'd found the papers the night before. It had the same kind of forgettable black-and-white tile floor, the same kind of forgettable light gray walls. But the other room had had a desk positioned right in the middle of the floor—the desk where the papers were hidden.

This room held no furniture at all.

"There's nothing here—let's go on," Eryn said anxiously.

She didn't know why it bothered her to see an empty room, but it did. Even the glaring light she'd longed for before was annoying to her now. Was it getting brighter? More overpowering? Could it blind her after so much darkness?

Ava just kept walking, farther and farther into the room. She reached the back wall and tugged on something Eryn hadn't noticed before, sticking out from the wall. A wire unspooled—a wire with a silver tip.

"The way this is designed—it would fit into the data port in my neck," Ava said, holding the wire up. She sounded like she was in a daze. Spellbound.

"Ava, *no*," Nick said. "That would be like . . . I don't know, like taking candy from a stranger. You don't know who left that wire there. You don't know why. Maybe it was the humans who wanted to *destroy* robots. Maybe it would *kill* you."

"But this is what I'm programmed to do," Ava said dreamily.

She shrugged off her backpack and dropped it to the floor.

And then she stuck the tip of the wire into her neck.

TWENTY-THREE

Ava

"Ava!" Eryn and Nick both screamed, rushing toward her.

Ava heard their cries as if they were miles away. Maybe it was only her enhanced hearing that let her hear them at all.

"Should we just pull it out?" Nick asked.

"What if *that* hurts her?" Eryn asked. "You know how you're not supposed to pull a flash drive out of a computer without ejecting it first . . ."

"I'm fine," Ava told them. It sounded like she was talking underwater. But that didn't worry her. She let herself sink down into a sitting position, leaning against the wall. "Everything's fine. Let me see what this tells me."

Eryn and Nick kept hovering, but they didn't reach down to yank the wire away. And then Ava stopped seeing them. Instead she saw a scene of a peaceful neighborhood. It had to be springtime in the image unfolding

in her mind, because tulips and daffodils were just bud-
ding, and the trees were bursting with new green leaves.
In front of one house, a man mowed his yard; beside
another, a woman planted a garden. And somehow Ava
knew that both of those people were robots. It was like
the wire planted that notion in her brain without words,
without effort.

"Humans used to live with a *lot* of robots," Ava told
Eryn and Nick. "Just about any job humans wanted
done—robots could do it for them."

Suddenly a row of tanks and Humvees thundered
onto the quiet street. Soldiers in ragtag camouflage
began firing on the man mowing the lawn, the woman
planting the garden. They fired into houses; Ava saw a
maid robot fall, a cook robot fall, a refrigerator-repairman
robot fall.

"Humans killed their robots!" Ava shrieked. "They
killed all their peaceful, hardworking robots. . . ."

"Ava, Ava—it was because robots were killing *them*,
remember?" Nick said. "The soldier robots they created
to fight their wars for them got out of control and started
killing *everyone*! Humans had to fight back!"

"But *these* robots never hurt anybody!" Ava protested. "They were faithful servants!"

She could feel tears streaming down her face. It was too awful watching the deaths of so many innocents. Incredibly, a wounded maid robot managed to struggle back to her feet. Rather than hiding or trying to save her own life, she shoved her way out the front door of her house, out into the open of the achingly green lawn.

"Please!" she called to the soldiers in their tanks and Humvees. "Please, I beg of you—stop! We mean no harm to anyone, neither robot nor human. We exist only to serve!"

"Lying robot!" one of the soldiers screamed back at her. He trained his gun on her; everyone else in his Humvee did the same. They fired and fired and fired.

The maid robot fell again. This time she didn't get back up.

"We know your kind are sneaky!" one of the soldiers yelled at her, at the whole neighborhood of dead and dying robots. "You can change your programming any-time you want . . . any of you can become killers!"

Is that true? Ava wondered. She and Jackson had enhanced their sight and hearing, and they'd extended the storage capacity of their brains. But they'd never tin-kered with their basic programming. Could they? Could any robot?

I don't want to be a killer, she thought with a shiver, watching more and more soldiers shooting more and more robots. *But could I really change who I am? Could I be stronger? Wiser? Better?*

"Ava—what do you see happening now?" Eryn shouted at her.

Ava didn't answer. It was impossible to describe the carnage she was watching. So much killing. So much death.

But then the scene changed. Now she was watching a small cluster of robots in a dark room.

"We have to hide, or face total extinction," a tall female robot said. "This isn't a battle we can win. No human will listen to reason anymore. They're all too afraid. They'll never trust us again."

"But where?" a man asked. His voice was heavy with despair. "Humans are present on virtually every part of the planet. Are you proposing we build a rocket ship and secretly launch ourselves into outer space? We couldn't hide that!"

"I'm not talking about outer space," the woman said. "I'm saying . . . let's hide where they're hiding. That would be the last place they'd look."

"What?" the man asked.

The woman produced paper maps and diagrams and began spreading them out on a table.

"Can't you just do a data transfer for all of us?" one of the other men complained.

"No," the woman said. "The humans are tracking things like that, just like we're tracking them. . . . Old-school is the only way to work this."

Ava realized that the maps on the table showed Mammoth Cave and the nature preserve around it.

"They're hiding frozen embryos here, for their future," the woman said, pointing at the exact center of one of the maps. "They think that's the only way to ensure their species continues after this war ends."

"You want to sneak in and destroy all their embryos, and replace them with robot parts, to rebuild *us* after the war?" one of the men said. "That's exactly the kind of thing they accuse us of—"

"*No,*" the woman said, showing a flash of anger. "I don't want to destroy anyone or anything. I want an end to all this destruction. I want to leave their embryos alone, and let them start over fresh. And I want us to be able to start over fresh. I want to store the . . . the seeds of our future elsewhere in that same cave. It's big—there's room for humans and robots. That way we can monitor what they're doing. Maybe add a few tweaks of our own. And then . . ."

"You think one day we can once again coexist peacefully?" a man asked, his voice ringing with doubt.

"I'm staking my life on it," the woman said. "Who's with me?"

Slowly, thoughtfully, everyone sitting around the table raised a hand. Even the doubtful man.

Ava watched months' worth of planning and strategizing. The handful of robots met secretly in basements and closed-down businesses even as bombs and gunfire sounded around them. And then she saw them walking among the trees, slipping into Mammoth Cave through an entrance she'd never seen before. She saw them tinker ever so slightly with the plans the humans had left behind for new caretaker robots to bring back humanity.

One of the changes left her sobbing all over again, when she finally understood what the humans had intended from the very beginning. What these robots were going to prevent.

One of the changes added an imperative for what to do if robots ever found themselves in a gray room with a black-and-white floor and a wire hanging out of the wall.

Is that a change that even I inherited? Ava wondered.

Is that why I felt so strongly that I had to link to this wire?

Then she saw the robots tinker with their own design, creating new robots who looked and acted less and less robotic, more and more like ordinary humans. Robots who, in fact, incorporated the backgrounds and memories of humans who had once lived near the cave.

One of those new robots was a girl with freckles and light brown braids. A girl who looked entirely human and wore old-fashioned clothes.

"Eryn! Nick!" Ava cried. "I know where Lida Mae came from now! Lida Mae's not human, after all! She's a robot like me!"

TWENTY-FOUR

Jackson

Jackson felt snow on his face. His eyelids fluttered; his vision swung in and out. He saw trees. Sky. More snow.

Nobody stood over him shaking his shoulders and shouting, *Jackson! Jackson! Wake up!*

This had never happened before—he had never awakened on his own after shorting out. His breakdowns had always required Mom or Dad or even Ava to unscramble his circuits or splice his wires and then do a total reboot.

But . . . maybe . . . maybe I could have rebooted on my own, if they'd ever just left me alone and let me try, Jackson thought groggily. *At least some of the time.*

Was that possible?

Jackson tried to remember why there *wasn't* someone standing over him. First he needed to recall what had happened right before he collapsed—always a tricky proposition.

The van . . . the cops . . . running and dragging Dad . . .
falling . . . Dad landing on top of me . . . Dad . . .

Where was Dad?

Jackson blinked, scattering the snowflakes caught
in his eyelashes. He tried to muster the energy to turn
his head and look around for Dad. It was a good thing
he didn't just try to move his whole body right away,
because a voice sounded off to the side: "Tell me how
any of this makes sense, Sergeant."

It was the female cop.

Jackson risked darting his eyes to the side, but only
his eyes. It was good that he'd enhanced the range of his
peripheral vision too. That meant he could see both the
male and female cop standing side by side, and Dad's
body stretched out on the ground before them.

They found us! he thought, fighting panic. He could
feel his circuits threatening to sizzle and zap out again,
but he struggled against the sensation. *As long as they
think you're still unconscious, you're fine. Just . . . listen.*

The male cop let out a heavy sigh.

"The first part of it seems obvious, doesn't it?" he
asked. "Kid looks about the right age. He's *not* human,
after all, but a kid almost due for . . . you know. The dad
couldn't bear it, blah, blah, blah, he went through the

usual channels, he wanted to hide his son . . ."

What? Jackson thought. It was true that Dad had brought Jackson—and Ava—to the nature preserve to hide, but how would the cop know that? What did he mean by "you know"? Or "the usual channels"?

"But why was the kid driving the van?" the female cop asked. "Why draw attention to himself? Why did he run off dragging his father?"

Oh no—did *they see me running?* Jackson wondered. It hardly mattered now. But it bothered him that he'd felt so confident he was out of sight when he really wasn't.

"And why are they both unconscious?" the male cop asked.

Jackson saw the cops glance his way, so he froze in place. He kept his eyelids at half-mast. Snow blew into his eyes, and he let the flakes brush right against his cornea.

"Should we take them back to the station to find out?" the female cop said. "Or just . . ."

"It's your call, boss," the male cop said. "Glad it's you and not me who has to write up this incident report."

"We always face the question of how much to keep secret," the female cop muttered.

Jackson's head spun, and he didn't think it was because he'd just awakened after falling. What were the cops keeping secret? And why? Even as a little kid in school, he'd learned that police officers did their jobs honestly and openly, enforcing every law as perfectly as they could. Later, once he'd learned that he and his sister were breaking a major law just by their very existence, Mom and Dad had explained that if the cops ever caught them, Ava and Jackson shouldn't be mad at the cops. The cops would just be doing their job. It would take someone at a higher level to see that it was really the law that was wrong, not Ava and Jackson.

The female cop put her hands on her hips and rocked back on her heels. The male cop cupped his chin in his hand. They seemed to be having a terrible time deciding what to do.

If it were just Jackson sprawled on the ground by himself, he would have jumped up and tried running away again. But he had Dad to worry about too. He couldn't abandon Dad. Could he grab Dad and then take off running? Would he make it more than two steps before the cops tackled him?

Who's to say I'm capable of running again anyway? Jackson wondered. More of his memory was coming back—he remembered not being able to move his arm. What if he really was paralyzed? What if he couldn't do anything but blink?

What if he had no choice at all about what happened to him next?

His brain ached. His innards twisted, as if his wiring and circuitry were tying themselves in knots. He felt woozy—exactly as if he was going to pass out again.

No! he told himself. *That can't happen!*

He heard a whimper escape from his throat.

Oh no, he told himself. *Don't be pathetic. If you're going to fail, go out in a blaze of glory.*

He made himself sit up. His left arm sagged uselessly, but his other muscles worked.

"I demand an attorney!" Jackson said. "I have rights! My life has value!"

Both cops turned to gape at him. They acted like they'd never heard such a request before. Their eyes grew to the size of quarters; their jaws dropped so far so fast they seemed in danger of scraping the ground.

"Do you . . . ," the female cop began. She cleared her throat and tried again. "Do you have any idea what you just set in motion?"

TWENTY-FIVE

Nick

"Lida Mae is a robot?" Nick repeated numbly. "Ava, how . . . why . . ."

But Ava didn't answer. She stayed completely still, her back against the wall, her eyes wide and vacant. Whatever trance she was in seemed unbreakable.

Eryn slugged Nick's arm.

"Nick, we're idiots!" she said. "Why didn't we think of that as a possibility? I mean, I did think she might be a robot when she first showed up, but as soon as I saw her eyes, as soon as I heard her speak . . ."

"Ava and Jackson don't look or sound much like robots either," Nick argued. "Not unless you pay really close attention. Or unless they break down. They're different kinds of robots from Mom and Dad. So . . . Lida Mae could be even more different."

"Why didn't we think about how the killer robots could have improved their technology too?" Eryn asked.

Her face suddenly turned three shades paler. "Oh no, the *killer* robots . . ."

"Ava, did Lida Mae come from the leftover killer robots?" Nick shouted at his stepsister, down on the floor. "Is she a killer robot, too, who just hasn't . . . acted yet?"

Ava still didn't answer. If it was possible, her face looked even blanker than before.

Eryn clutched Nick's arm. Maybe Nick clutched hers, too. He wasn't thinking very clearly.

"Eryn, we've got to—we've got to—" he stammered.

Eryn looked over her shoulder toward the door, as if she expected a whole horde of killer robots to come stomping in.

"Lida Mae's out there chasing Mom and Dad and Brenda," Eryn said. Now she was practically shaking.

"But they're safe. From her, anyway," Nick said. "Because they're robots. Killer robots only kill humans. Don't they?"

"But does *she* know they're robots?" Eryn asked. "What if she thinks . . . she thinks . . . We've got to go save them!"

Eryn yanked on Nick's arm, pulling him toward the door.

"But, Ava . . . we can't leave Ava . . . ," Nick protested.

"They'll know she's a robot because she's sitting there *plugged in*!" Eryn said. "Come on!"

She pulled harder on Nick's arm.

"Ava!" Nick shouted. "We've got to go rescue Mom and Dad. And your mom! Maybe even Jackson and your dad, too! Come with us!"

Ava still didn't answer. Eryn tugged Nick practically over to the door. He gave in and ran with her. But when he reached the door, he resisted again. He hesitated just long enough to slide his fingers under the FOR ROBOT ACCESS ONLY sign and yank it off the door. He dropped it to the ground. Then he pulled the door shut behind him.

"That way . . . that way they won't recognize this room anymore," he gasped to Eryn. "They'll stay out. Ava will be safe."

Eryn just kept running.

TWENTY-SIX

Ava

Ava looked up, and Nick and Eryn were gone.

They're safe as long as they stay in the cave, she thought. *They know to stay in the cave. Because Lida Mae told them.*

She went back to absorbing all the robot history she'd never known.

TWENTY-SEVEN

Eryn

Eryn's backpack thudded up and down, beating against her spine. Her breath came in ragged gasps. She was used to running on a basketball court or soccer field, but not in such a full-out sprint for such a long distance. Was this cave endless? How could it seem like they'd been running for hours to get out of the cave, when they'd only walked for ten or fifteen minutes to get into it?

And how could the walls keep getting closer and closer together, rather than opening out into the huge entryway?

What might Lida Mae be doing to Mom and Dad right now, while Nick and Eryn just kept running and running to rescue them?

"Do—you—think—" Nick panted beside her. "Maybe—we went—the wrong way? Back—where—the trail—split?"

Eryn skidded to a halt. Pebbles slid under her feet and she almost fell.

"What do you mean . . . the trail split?" She gulped for air. It was hard to get more than two or three words out at a time. "It was a straight path in! It should be a straight path out!"

Nick shook his head, the motion barely detectable outside the main glow of the flashlight.

"There was a fork back there," he said, gesturing toward the darkness behind them. "We probably didn't see it coming in, because of the angle. You were ahead of me when we got to it this time, and you just kept running, so I thought you knew what you were doing."

"I didn't see there was a choice!" Eryn fumed. "I couldn't see. . . ." She yanked the flashlight out of Nick's hand and shone it all around. "We weren't anywhere before where the passageway was this narrow! Nowhere before had such a low ceiling! Nick, we're lost!"

"We just have to retrace our steps," Nick said. "We'll be fine."

"But will Mom and Dad?" Eryn asked.

She started to whirl around, sending the beam of the flashlight into a crazy arc. It shone to the right, to the front, to the ceiling, to the left . . .

Nick grabbed her arm, steadying the flashlight and

sending its beam back into the thick darkness directly ahead of them.

"Wait, Eryn—doesn't it look like the cave opens out ahead of us?" he asked. "Maybe we *did* go the right way, and we just didn't notice this one narrow section before. Maybe we just have to keep going. . . ."

Tugging on Eryn's arm, he took another step forward. The flashlight beam *did* illuminate a much higher ceiling ahead of them, but that still didn't convince Eryn they were going the right way. She hated not knowing.

"Well, let's look fast, and then if it's not the right way, we'll turn around," Eryn said.

Now she was the one rushing Nick forward. She kept sweeping the light around in a pattern, looking up, down, right, left, ahead. The passageway kept widening, until they reached a point where the ceiling was so high overhead it was hard to see.

"Maybe *this* is that Rotunda place Lida Mae was talking about," Nick suggested. "Maybe we got totally turned around when we left Ava."

"No, I'm sure we turned the right way then," Eryn insisted. "We—"

She swept the flashlight beam to the right, and it landed on a long row of . . .

"Are those *cribs*?" Nick asked, sounding spooked. "Is this . . . Is this the exact room where we were kept as babies?"

"*No*—we were just kept at Mammoth Cave as frozen embryos," Eryn corrected. "Remember? When it was time to restart humanity, they moved the embryos somewhere else. All over the planet. Once we were babies, we were always with Mom or Dad. We had a home."

It was hard just to say "Mom or Dad." Or "home."

"But . . . ," Nick began.

He didn't have to go on. Eryn knew he was going to say, *But look at all those cribs! Somebody had babies in them! Lots and lots of babies . . .*

The row of cribs stretched on and on, past the range of the flashlight beam, even after Eryn stepped forward and held the flashlight out farther.

"Is there something on the other side of all those cribs?" Nick asked. His voice dropped to a whisper. "Something . . . hiding?"

The question gave Eryn chills, and she wanted to turn around and run back to Mom and Dad. But now she wanted them to help her, rather than her to help them. She wanted them to brush her messy hair away from her face and pat her on the back and say, *There,*

there. Everything's going to be okay. . . . You're just imagining that anyone's in danger. . . .

She wasn't imagining the dangers around her. But she didn't understand them either. And if she was going to rescue anyone—herself or Nick or their parents—she needed to know what was going on.

She took a step toward the row of cribs and the dark shadows behind them.

"Let's go look together," she muttered to Nick, reaching for his arm. "We'll be safe as long as we're together."

That wasn't logical, but it made her feel better to hold on to him.

She lifted the flashlight higher, trying to arc the beam into the nearest crib.

"These cribs *were* for babies," Nick breathed. "That one's still got a baby in it!"

Eryn stifled a scream. Nick was right. The crib in front of them held a tiny form under a pink blanket. The infant's head was turned to the side, its rosy face framed by curly dark hair, a tiny thumb pressed against the bottom lip. But the baby didn't move; the portion of the blanket covering the chest didn't rise and fall with any rhythmic breathing.

"Is it . . . is it *dead*?" Nick whispered.

Eryn whipped the flashlight beam from the one motionless baby in the crib in front of them, to the next crib, and the next one, and the one after that. They all contained babies, too.

"No," Eryn said, her voice harsh and raspy. "It was never alive. Not really. It's a robot baby. They all are. And those back there"—she moved the flashlight past the row of cribs, to the shadowy shapes beyond—"those are robot children. This is a roomful of robots waiting to take over!"

TWENTY-EIGHT

Jackson

"Do I have any idea what I just set in motion?" Jackson repeated the female cop's words back to her. "I *believe* I was just asking for my Miranda warning rights. You know, I have the right to remain silent, I have the right to an attorney . . ."

He let his voice trail off, because the cops weren't reacting right. They both still looked stunned. Flabbergasted.

Maybe even scared.

"We—we weren't arresting you," the female cop managed to stammer.

"Oh. Then I'm free to go?" Jackson asked. He would have stood up if he'd felt sure his legs wouldn't tremble or collapse. He did shake the snow out of his hair. He hoped the motion looked defiant and confident.

The two cops exchanged glances.

"There are too many oddities here to just let him

go," the male cop muttered. "His father's *unconscious*."

"And he asked for an attorney," the female cop sighed.

"I could take it back, if you just let me and Dad go," Jackson offered.

Both cops ignored him.

"Let's revive the dad and see what he has to say for himself," the male cop suggested. "What he remembers."

No! Jackson wanted to scream. If the cops scanned Dad's memories, they'd see that he and Mom had created Ava and Jackson illegally. They'd see that Ava, Mom, and the rest of his stepfamily were hiding out at the campsite up by the entrance to Mammoth Cave.

They'd arrest everyone.

"You—you can't do that," Jackson managed to stammer. "Dad shut himself down before . . . before we came here. So it wouldn't do any good for you to check his memories. He doesn't remember anything about the last half hour."

The female cop's eyebrows shot up practically to her hairline.

"*That's* a new strategy," she said.

"Maybe he's telling the truth," the male cop said.

"We had to expect the plotting to evolve constantly. And the kids in question *are* getting older."

Jackson had no idea what they were talking about. But at least they weren't dismissing everything he said.

"If only he hadn't asked for a lawyer," the female cop said, shaking her head sadly.

"What's wrong with asking for a lawyer?" Jackson asked.

"Paperwork," she answered. "Records. Proof. Attention."

Jackson felt dizzy all over again. He gulped in air.

"We can't stand out here in the snow forever trying to figure this out," the male cop pointed out, glancing toward the sky.

"I know," the female cop said. "You're right."

The snowflakes were blowing sideways now. Jackson wondered if some of the snow had blown into his circuit casing. That would make it even harder to fix his bum arm.

I should have told them Dad's circuits were blown by the snow, Jackson scolded himself.

But they would have figured out the truth as soon as they tried to reboot him.

What am I going to do? he wondered. *What can I*

do to keep them from scanning all of Dad's memories?

"Come on, kid," the male cop said, pulling on Jackson's good arm to get him to stand up. "Let's get a move on. You walk, and Lieutenant Kapowski and I will carry your dad. If you try any funny business, we'll drop him and chase you."

"Don't drop my dad. You won't have to chase me," Jackson mumbled.

Numbly, he walked alongside the cops back through the trees, back to the highway. It was hard to see where they were going in the snow, which was blowing around more and more.

"Bet they'll be shutting down the highway soon," the female cop shouted, over the shrieking wind.

"Good we're getting out now," the male cop shouted back.

They shoved Jackson into the backseat of the squad car and slid Dad's slumped-over body in beside him.

"Back to the police station, and *then* we'll check the dad's memories," the female cop said. "I bet his memories will be more interesting than the kid thinks."

You don't know the half of it, Jackson thought miserably.

"Sorry, Dad," he whispered, even though he knew

Dad couldn't hear. "You were counting on me and I . . . I failed."

Dad's body flopped against Jackson's as though the framework of his body had rusted out.

Wish his memory units had rusted out instead, Jackson thought. *Wish I could blank it all out before the police revive him and scan his brain.*

Wait—wasn't there a way that Jackson could do that?

Right, and everything about Dad would be gone. His memories, his personality, his programming . . .

What if Jackson backed up all that in his own brain before erasing Dad's mind? The combined power of Jackson's mind plus Dad's would be able to figure out an escape. And then when they were away from the cops, Jackson could upload Dad's memories back to Dad's head.

Jackson realized he was still clutching the bag of electronic parts. He shook melting snow off the sack and pulled out a cord.

"Dad, I really do know what I'm doing," he whispered, mostly just to reassure himself.

The cops were sliding into the front seat now. The female reached for the police radio.

"Returning to station," she reported. "Confirm. Over."

Jackson cared only that they weren't looking back at him. He snaked a cord from the back of his neck to the back of Dad's and tucked it into his coat, so the cops wouldn't be able to see it even if they turned around.

"Download all," he whispered.

He felt a jolt. Images swam in his head of Dad's long, secret nights in the computer lab. Of Dad scanning long lists of rules and regulations and figuring out how to evade them all. Then Jackson watched himself and Ava as babies, as toddlers, as gap-toothed first graders. It was so weird to watch events Jackson remembered—a soccer game where Jackson scored the winning goal, a second-grade music program where Jackson played a giraffe—entirely from Dad's perspective.

How could I have understood so little about how much he loves us? Jackson wondered. *About how much he was fighting? About how he risked everything for us from the very day we were conceived?*

This was not the moment to get sentimental.

Dad's memories downloaded in order, so Jackson knew they were near the end when he began seeing scenes of the nature preserve. He saw his immediate family—plus his step-relatives—hiking into the nature preserve the day before. He saw the whole group in the cave. Then he saw himself and Dad hiking out of the nature preserve.

Then the memory arrived where Dad had stepped out of the nature preserve and reconnected to the robot network. Jackson felt the same kind of shock Dad had felt when the new, dangerous information seared through his circuits.

Oh no, Jackson thought. *Oh no . . .*

He struggled to stay conscious. But it wasn't enough just to stay alert—he had to *act.* Now.

Fortunately, combining Dad's knowledge with his own meant that he knew more about his options. He jerked the cord out of his neck and dug deeper into the bag of electronic parts. Wires, circuit boards, microchips . . . He worked in a rush, shoving new parts into his stomach, using his coat as a shield to keep the cops from seeing what he was doing, even if they turned around.

Then he was done.

"This is what I've got to do," he whispered into his father's ear. "I think even you would agree it's the only choice. I have to warn the others."

With newly installed superhuman strength, he flung open the locked car door beside him. He hadn't noticed that, while he'd been working, the car had pulled back onto the highway and was accelerating toward the speed limit—past thirty miles per hour, past thirty-five, past forty . . .

It didn't matter. Yanking seat belts from their moorings and casting them aside, Jackson grabbed his father around the waist and sprang out of the car.

And then, still carrying his father, Jackson took off running back toward the nature preserve.

TWENTY-NINE

Nick

Nick stared at the row of motionless babies in cribs, at the rows of motionless toddlers and preschoolers and elementary school kids behind them. Eryn had to be right; they had to be robots. No humans could stay that still without being dead. For all Nick knew, these robots might have been here for decades, for centuries, totally unchanging. Lying in wait.

Eryn kept running the flashlight beam back and forth over the rows and rows of robots.

"You really believe . . . ," Nick whispered. "That they're . . . they're . . ."

"Think about it," Eryn said. Even completely horrified, she was still his take-charge sister. She could still sound so certain. "Think about what we already know. The killer robots had one purpose—to kill humans. They weren't programmed to notice embryos as humans. We know that from the papers we found in the secret room—and from the fact that we're alive at all. So centuries ago, once they'd killed all the humans who were babies or older, the killer robots probably thought they'd done everything they needed to. They didn't have any other reason to exist. So maybe they decided to shut down to, I don't know, conserve energy until they felt they were 'needed' again. And they didn't know that the human race was starting up again outside this cave. . . ."

"Lida Mae wasn't shut down," Nick pointed out.

"How do you know she wasn't, before we showed up in the cave?" Eryn asked. "What if she was, like, the early-warning sentry or something, and she was just reactivated when we tripped some sensor showing there were humans in the area?"

Nick hated it that Eryn's theory sounded so logical. So plausibly robotlike. He wanted to find a hole in her reasoning so he could pick the whole thing apart.

"Lida Mae hasn't tried to kill any of us," he protested.

"That we know of," Eryn said despairingly. "Yet. Maybe she's waiting to find out how many humans there are out in the rest of the world. Maybe when she finds that out, she'll . . . she'll . . ."

Nick could tell that his sister was trying not to follow her thoughts to their logical end. She had to be thinking about Mom and Dad and Brenda, out there in the snow with Lida Mae chasing them.

The grown-ups didn't know *anything*. Because Lida Mae didn't look or act like a regular robot—and had never been part of their robot network—they didn't even know to be suspicious.

Nick expected his sister to spin around and shout, *Come on! We don't have time to stand here staring! We've got to go rescue Mom and Dad!*

But Eryn just kept standing there, running her flashlight beam across one robot face after another. All the robots Nick could see were babies or children—younger children than him and Eryn, even. Did that mean they'd been designed to seem cute and cuddly and harmless, right up until the moment that they killed you?

Nick felt sick to his stomach just thinking about that.

"About Mom and Dad . . . ," he hinted. It would help to throw his energy into running and running and running, so he wouldn't have to look at or think about all these robots.

Eryn frowned, held up one hand, and shook her head, which Nick took to mean, *I know! I know! But I want to make sure we're doing this right. . . .*

"You haven't changed your mind," Nick said, his

voice coming out cold and flat. "You are *not* thinking now that we do have to kill all the robots. Even our own parents."

"*No*," Eryn said. Her hand was a fist now. "There *are* different kinds of robots. The ones like Mom and Dad—they aren't evil. We have to protect them. I think maybe we're the only ones who can protect them. But I'm trying to think strategically. If we go out and destroy Lida Mae, maybe that just activates the next robot. And then if we destroy that robot, the next one comes alive. So . . . I think we have to start with the robots that are all asleep."

She handed him the flashlight, then bent down and picked up a small column of rock about the length of a baseball bat. Maybe it was a stalagmite or a stalactite that someone had carelessly knocked to the floor.

"Hold the light steady," Eryn told Nick. Her voice shook. She stepped up to the nearest crib.

"I have to do this," Eryn whispered to herself, raising the rock column over her head. "I have to, to protect my family. I have to, to save all of humanity."

Nick flinched, and closed his eyes. He couldn't watch. He wasn't programmed like a robot, but he'd been raised to avoid violence. He'd been raised to think through options and possibilities before choosing an action. Sometimes he disobeyed; sometimes he misbehaved. But he got a little squeamish even slapping a mosquito. The truth was, he wasn't as brave as Eryn.

Or is it that I'm not as rash?

Nick opened his eyes. Eryn was just starting to swing the rock column. He reached out and grabbed her arm.

"Stop!" he yelled. "What if you're wrong?"

THIRTY

Ava

Ava felt like she knew everything now. Everything about the history of robots; everything about the tragic history of humans and robots together.

Everything her predecessors had hoped was possible for the future.

Thoughtfully, she pulled the wire out of her brain stem and coiled it up again along the wall of the gray room. The wire's tip was the kind that could fit into a robot's brain or a laptop's port. Once that would have humiliated her—made her feel like just another pathetic machine. But she wasn't ashamed of being a robot anymore. Now she understood why that shame had been built in to her programming. It was because so much dated back to the original humans and their attitudes—their fear of being surpassed by robots.

Even though *she'd* been designed by her parents, *they'd* been designed by humans. And they hadn't been able to completely disregard their programming or their basic beliefs.

But it was possible to change some beliefs and overcome the past.

It was.

Ava had so much to tell Mom and Dad and Jackson. And Donald and Denise, and even Eryn and Nick.

No, she thought. It felt like the new information in her brain was giving her a nudge. *I need to tell everyone. Every single robot and human on the entire planet.*

But first she needed to find Nick and Eryn.

She let her memory rewind a bit, listening to what she'd tuned out before. When Nick and Eryn left, what had they said? Oh yes: *We've got to go rescue Mom and Dad. And your mom! Maybe even Jackson and your dad, too!*

That meant they'd planned to leave the cave.

Ava brought up maps that were now imprinted on her memory, maps showing every inch of the cave in great detail. She saw exactly the route Nick and Eryn would have taken. She saw how they could have gotten lost—and *where* they might have gotten lost.

Oh no, Ava thought, scrambling up from the floor. *Oh no.*

What happened to Nick and Eryn next, and how they chose to respond—that could ruin everything. That could destroy all the careful plans and strategies that Ava's kind had taken centuries to put into place.

Ava stepped out of the room and peered back and forth, her enhanced vision taking in probably a quarter mile in either direction. Nick and Eryn were nowhere in sight. She did see that the FOR ROBOT ACCESS ONLY sign had fallen or been removed from the door. She paused long enough to put it back in place.

Then she took off running.

THIRTY-ONE

Jackson

Having superhuman strength and speed was *amazing*.

Even with Dad's body slung over his shoulder, Jackson felt like his feet barely touched ground as he sprinted away from the police car. It took only six steps before he was at the edge of the woods again. There was no danger of the cops catching him, because nobody else in the world could run as fast as Jackson was running now.

Heck, they couldn't even drive their car *as fast as I'm going now,* Jackson thought jubilantly, even though he didn't bother computing his actual velocity to be certain.

He was pretty sure the heavy snow hid him from sight already; the wind racing behind him probably erased his footprints a moment after he left them. Still, he kept running full speed into the woods. In the blink of an eye he passed the spot where he'd collapsed before. The place where he'd dropped Dad.

No way I'd drop him now, Jackson told himself. *I*

could carry him over my head in the palm of one hand. I could hold his entire weight on the tip of one finger!

But the reason Jackson had dropped his father before hadn't been weakness. It had been because Jackson had blacked out. And that could happen even with super-human strength and speed.

Jackson felt a lot less jubilant.

Stay calm, he reminded himself. *You're fine. But . . . strategize. Prepare an optimal plan for every possibility.*

As the snow swirled around him—as he made a vir-tual tornado in the snow, with his own speed—his mind raced even faster.

If I black out again, I can't leave both Dad and me totally defenseless, he thought. *The snow doesn't bother me now, but if we were both lying unconscious on the ground for hours, the snow would probably get into our circuitry and melt and refreeze and . . . that could kill us.*

He was still using the humancentric language he'd been taught by his human-loving parents. It wasn't really appropriate, now that he'd been upgraded in every way.

But leaving even a superhuman robot out in a bliz-zard like this would be like . . . like dropping a cell phone in a toilet and leaving it there for hours, Jackson told himself. It was the most humiliating comparison he could think of. He *had* accidentally knocked a phone into a toilet once, and even though Mom had put it in a bag of rice, it had never worked again.

What if he broke down and they lay in the snow for hours—and nobody could ever fix him or Dad, either?

That thought brought him completely down from his euphoria.

He began scanning the area ahead of him. The air was now so thick with snow that even with his enhanced vision he could barely see anything. He almost ran into a tree branch coated with snow; he clunked his toes against a rock hidden by a layer of white.

I've got to revive Dad and restore him, Jackson thought. *I can't wait until we're back with the others. I have to leave him a chance to rescue both of us, if I fall. Or fail.*

Up ahead Jackson saw a place where a rock overhang sheltered the ground beneath it from the worst of the snow. That could give him a relatively dry place to work. And even though it would probably take the cops with their normal skills an hour or two to cover the distance Jackson had just raced through in five minutes, the rock overhang would also hide Jackson from anyone who might be nearby.

He scaled the hillside without even breathing hard. But once he slid into the sheltered spot, his hands shook as he laid Dad's body out on the ground.

This is no different from restoring files on a computer, he told himself. But it was. This was his father's very essence—his soul, even, if Jackson could use such a human word. For Dad to be revived and restored to himself, every byte—no, every *bit*, every single one of the binary digits that had been contained in his brain—had to transfer back exactly right.

Jackson pulled out a cord again from the bag of supplies. He inspected it for chips and microscopic cracks. He plugged one end into his father's neck and the other into his own. He'd been so rushed before, in the car, but this time he checked and double-checked and triple-checked himself on every step. He stretched a two-second process into one lasting five minutes—he was that careful.

Finally there was nothing else to check.

"Restore full set of Michael Lightner's memories and programming from Jackson Lightner's head back into Michael Lightner's," Jackson said, making sure he enunciated each word perfectly. "But . . . don't delete copied files from Jackson Lightner's head."

Jackson told himself he was just being cautious. He needed to keep a backup copy of his dad's memories in case something went wrong.

Jackson felt a throbbing in his head that he hadn't noticed when he was making the transfer in the other direction. But he hadn't had superhuman strength then—maybe his greater athletic ability also gave him greater awareness of every detail of his body.

The throbbing ended.

"Reboot Michael Lightner," Jackson said. "Revive him."

Dad's eyelids began to flutter.

"Denise?" he called weakly. "Brenda? Donald?"

It annoyed Jackson that Dad called for the adults first—as if Dad assumed it would have taken their help to bring him back.

Still, Jackson made his voice gentle when he said, "No, Dad, they're not here. We're headed back that way, but we're not there yet. I stopped and rebooted you now because . . ."

Dad raised up on his elbows. He gazed out at the thick snow blowing sideways across the opening of their shelter. Jackson turned to look in the same direction.

Even with his advanced eyes, he couldn't see anything but snow past the nearest tree.

"Of course," Dad murmured. "You've got to be terrified. You need me to take care of you."

"Dad, I'm *fine*," Jackson protested. "We're fine. Mostly. I'm just being strategic. But . . . why didn't you tell me? Why did you keep so many secrets when we were both in danger, when . . ."

Dad peered at the cord still connecting him and Jackson.

"You downloaded my memories?" Dad asked, jerking back. The cord popped out of its socket, breaking the link between them. "You know . . . ?"

"Dad, I had to," Jackson said, and he didn't even sound defensive, just matter-of-fact. "It's a long story, but I thought I was doing the right thing. Now I know everything you know. I know *more*, because a lot happened in the hour you were unconscious."

Dad started to open his mouth, but Jackson didn't wait for him to speak.

"That doesn't mean I understand," Jackson said. Now he sounded bitter. "You should have told me before, how the original humans wanted to phase out all robots. And that the restarted humans are supposed to completely replace us. And that *that's* the biggest reason Ava and I are illegal, that's the reason it's wrong that we can grow and change, and—"

"I never thought you'd *need* to know!" Dad protested. "I always thought you two would be the best proof that robots and humans could coexist just fine! Forever! I always thought everything would work out in time. . . ."

Dad grimaced and peered out at the blinding snow. It seemed cruel to keep accusing him, but Jackson couldn't help himself.

"You should have told me what you found out when you first stepped out of the nature preserve," Jackson said. "When you reconnected with the robot network."

"You mean that I heard an all-call," Dad said, his voice flat and emotionless. He looked back at Jackson, his face blank. "An all-call for information pertaining to you, me, Ava, your mom, Denise, and Donald. But not Nick or Eryn."

Jackson hadn't thought about how the all-call list had omitted the human members of his family.

"Right," he said. He leaned closer to his father, beseechingly. "And, Dad, you always told me that no robot could resist an all-call for information. You told me that if any other robot asked for information about a particular subject, and you knew anything at all about that subject, you *had* to respond."

"That," his father said faintly, "is the exact definition of an all-call. An all-call for our information . . . that's the very thing we've feared most ever since you and Ava were born."

"But somehow you managed to resist!" Jackson said, still stunned. Awe overcame the accusing tone in his voice. "You ignored the all-call when you were standing in the ditch, and the whole time we were driving to that store. And the whole time you were *in* the store. Why didn't you just jump back into the nature preserve, the first hint you got that there might be an all-call? Why did you still go on to the store? How did you possibly resist a call that no robot *can* resist?"

He knew the answer. But somehow he still wanted to hear Dad say it.

"Because I love you," Dad whispered. "You *needed* those parts from the store. And . . . if I'd answered that all-call, the authorities would have destroyed you. I *had* to resist."

Jackson started shaking his head.

"Oh, Dad," he moaned. "The problem is, I didn't

know why you'd shut yourself down. And . . . I blacked out and the cops caught us. And I ran away, but I'm sure they're going to come looking for us. Eventually. We've got to find a better place for the whole family to hide."

"The cops *caught* us?" Dad repeated numbly. He whipped his head side to side, as if he expected to see a bunch of men and women in uniform appearing out of the snow. "And they IDed me, and they still let you get away?"

"Oh," Jackson said, jerking back and hitting his head against the rock. This was an element he hadn't thought of. "Maybe they didn't ID you. Because when they found us, we were in the nature preserve, where they couldn't link to the network. And then when they carried you out of the woods, to put us in their car . . . I guess they weren't paying attention? Because of the snow?"

"That doesn't make sense," Dad said. "Everyone linked to the network pays attention to the network all the time."

"Well, then, those cops . . . uh . . . They did mention keeping secrets," Jackson said. But he was as mystified as his father.

"But . . ." Dad seemed to be thinking hard.

"Dad, I don't think there's time to figure all this out,"

Jackson said. "I think we need to go find the others. And hide."

Stiffly, Dad started pushing himself up.

"Are you . . . feeling shaky?" Dad asked. "Do you need me to carry you?"

"No, Dad," Jackson said. He knew everything his father knew, and that meant he knew exactly how much danger they were in. Jackson had to reveal his newest secret, if they had any hope of surviving. "I went through some . . . changes . . . while you were shut down. I think it's best if I carry you. Want to climb onto my back?"

Dad shot him a puzzled look but wrapped his arms around Jackson's neck. Jackson held on to Dad's knees. A burst of nostalgia flared in Jackson's brain, and he realized it was from one of Dad's memories, not his own.

This piggyback style was exactly how Dad had carried Jackson when Jackson was little.

Jackson pushed the memory and the emotion aside and took off running at top speed out into the snow.

THIRTY-TWO

Eryn

"What if these aren't a bunch of killer robots, ready to murder us all?" Nick asked. "What if these are just a bunch of . . . innocent kids?"

Eryn slumped, letting the rock column she was holding sag to the floor.

"How can we know?" she whispered. "I don't want to kill—or destroy—anyone. But we have to protect ourselves. And we have to protect all the rest of the people in the world, all the *human* kids who are younger than us, who don't even know there are robots passing themselves off as human. . . . What if we're the only ones who can save humanity?"

"I think we probably are," Nick whispered back. "But . . . what if we do something that ends up causing humanity to be destroyed all over again? And this time there's no backup plan?"

Eryn winced. Why was this so hard? She felt tears

threaten at her eyes, and she wasn't sure if it was because she'd almost destroyed an innocent baby or because she still thought she might need to. Or because she maybe still wanted to?

Eryn didn't let herself cry.

"Tell me any other possible reason for these rows of robot babies and kids to be here," she challenged. "Why would anyone leave robots behind in this cave *except* as killers?"

"Maybe they're . . . they're robot kids who are going to be stand-ins for human kids," Nick said. "Remember how everything worked with the plan for humanity to start up again? Remember how all the kids who are older than us are actually robots, and we never knew it?"

"Right—it's kids *older* than us who are always the placeholders," Eryn said. "We're in the oldest group of the new generation of humanity. Michael told us about how the year we turned one, all the one-year-old robots were taken away and destroyed. The year we turned two, all the two-year-old robots were taken away and destroyed. And so on. Once there were human babies and toddlers and elementary school kids, no one needed placeholder robots of those ages. So there aren't supposed to be *any* robot kids our age or younger ever again. That's how the plan works."

"Except, Michael and Brenda—and Mom and Dad—broke the rules by creating Ava and Jackson," Nick said. "They're the same age as us. They've grown up the same as us, instead of staying one age their whole life." He gazed out at the rows and rows of robots. "Maybe lots of robot adults are breaking the rules and creating new children."

Without even thinking about it, Eryn tightened her grip on the stone column.

"Innocent, nonkiller robot children, I mean," Nick added quickly. "Maybe these kids were created just because . . . well, you know how Michael explained Jackson and Ava. He said all the grown-ups were programmed to love being parents. So they wanted to raise kids who were robots like them, not just kids who were humans. Maybe there were other parents who did that too. And maybe those parents just haven't figured out yet how to . . . bring their kids out of the cave yet. Into normal life."

It seemed like Nick was trying to convince her that these were innocent and harmless robots in front of them. But every word he said made her see the rows of robots more and more like an army in the making. An army that could destroy humans.

"Nobody was supposed to know about this cave!" Eryn said. "We looked up the GPS coordinates and it said there was nothing here! How could so many people—so many *robots*—be storing kids here without anyone finding out? How could so many robots defy their programming? Remember how upset Michael got talking about how all the kid robots younger than us have been melted down for scrap? And how the thirteen-year-old robots are next? The robots couldn't even defy their programming to stop that!"

Nick gasped. And then he threw himself at Eryn, and wrapped his arms around her.

"Eryn—you're a genius!" he said. "Or . . . we are together. You just helped me figure out everything!"

"I did?" Eryn asked, pulling back. She shot her gaze back and forth between Nick and the rows of robots. "What did I say?"

"You said the robot parents couldn't stop the robot kids younger than us from being melted down for scrap," Nick said. "But what if they actually could? What if *that's* who all of these robot babies and kids are? The ones who were supposed to be destroyed?"

THIRTY-THREE

Ava

Ava could hear Nick's and Eryn's voices ahead of her in the dark cave long before she could see them. She heard Nick say, "What if these aren't a bunch of killer robots, ready to murder us all?" and she dared to ease up her pace a little. They weren't doing anything rash; they were thinking and talking. Then she heard Eryn ask, "What if we're the only ones who can save humanity?" and "Why would anyone leave robots behind in this cave *except* as killers?" and she started running her fastest once again.

Even at top speed, Ava tried to step as silently as possible—wouldn't Nick and Eryn freak out even worse if they heard footsteps thundering toward them?

Ava was just entering the narrow part of the passageway when she heard Nick spring his theory about the robot babies and children being ones rescued from destruction, and she was so happy that she shouted out, "Yes, Nick! That's exactly what they are!"

"Ava?" Eryn called. Just from her tone, Ava could picture how Eryn would be standing: staunchly, her back straight, her face rigid, as if any of that would help hide her terror.

Ava realized she shouldn't have shouted from so far away.

Did Nick speak loudly enough that someone with normal ears could have heard him at this distance? she wondered. *Will they think I've been lurking behind them all along, eavesdropping?*

"Ava, where are you?" Nick called.

"Almost there!" Ava yelled back, trying to throw her voice to make it sound like she wasn't so far away.

She sped through the rest of the passageway and came out into the vast open space with the rows and rows of cribs and kids. Eryn directed her flashlight beam straight at Ava's face, temporarily blinding her.

"Ava?" Eryn called doubtfully. "Did you lose your flashlight? Did your batteries die?"

Oh no, Ava thought. She couldn't remember where she'd left the flashlight. She hadn't needed it, and she'd been in such a hurry. Was it back on the floor of the FOR ROBOT ACCESS ONLY room? With her backpack, which she'd also left behind?

"Lost it," Ava said. Automatically, she patted the pockets of her coat. There was a solid lump inside that wasn't mittens. "Oh, here it is. I mean . . ."

Eryn lowered her flashlight a little, and now Ava could see the skeptical squint plastered across her step-sister's face. Nick held onto Eryn's arm. His expression wasn't exactly trusting either.

Ava sighed and made a quick decision.

"Actually," she said, "Jackson and I both upgraded our eyes so they can work like night-vision goggles anytime we want. We . . . we got kind of bored some-times when Mom was homeschooling us and we weren't allowed to hang out with other kids. So that was some-thing fun to play around with. We just . . . kept it secret so our parents wouldn't get mad. Please don't tell."

Eryn's face went even more rigid.

Ava pulled the flashlight from her pocket and held it out toward Nick.

"Here," Ava said. "Now you can both have your own light. I, uh, I'm glad you two figured out who these robot kids are. I thought you might be afraid of them and do something . . . crazy."

Nick took the flashlight from Ava and glanced quickly back at Eryn. Eryn pursed her lips.

I bet Eryn almost did do something crazy, Ava thought. *I bet she would have, if Nick hadn't stopped her. And . . . she still might.*

"Jackson and I never knew the rules about younger robots being destroyed," Ava said. It felt like she was chattering away again. But this was important. She had to make Nick and Eryn understand. "Mom and Dad always glossed over that part of the original humans' plan. I . . . I'm glad I didn't find out until I was in the FOR ROBOT ACCESS ONLY ROOM. And about two seconds later, I found out that the rules were always disobeyed."

Nick shone his flashlight beam over the rows and rows of babies and kids.

"So *none* of the kids younger than us were ever destroyed?" he said. "Just . . . shut down and hidden?"

"That's right," Ava said. "Lida Mae's ancestors changed the way the caretaker robots—our parents' generation—were programmed."

She saw Nick and Eryn dart their eyes at each other again.

"So your dad was lying when he told us about little-kid robots being killed?" Eryn asked. Her voice came out angry and harsh. "He made up that whole story to trick us, and make us sad, and get our sympathy, and—"

"*No,*" Ava said. "I mean, I don't know exactly what Dad told you, but I'm sure he thought all the baby and little-kid robots *were* destroyed. And it's not like it's great for robots to be left in storage for years. Lida Mae's ancestors couldn't make too many changes in the programming, so they left people thinking that the rules were being followed. And then . . ."

"I don't understand," Nick said flatly. "I don't think I understand robots at all."

"Well, I didn't either, until now," Ava assured him. "Do you want to hear what else I learned back in that room?"

"Only if you tell us while we're going after Mom and Dad, to rescue them from Lida Mae," Eryn said. Her expression was still tight and unfriendly.

"Eryn, listen, Lida Mae's not a danger to anyone," Ava said. "She—"

"I'll feel better if I can see that for myself," Eryn said, interrupting. "If I can see Mom and Dad aren't in danger."

"Even if it means risking your own life in a blizzard?" Ava asked.

"Yes!" Eryn insisted.

"Eryn gets like this, sometimes," Nick said, almost as if he were apologizing. "She's stubborn."

Ava gave him a look that she hoped he'd read as *Can't you talk sense into your sister?* Even if Lida Mae were dangerous, she'd be more of a threat to Nick and Eryn than their parents. Couldn't they see that? It was simple logic.

But then Nick added, "And . . . I'd like to make sure they're okay too."

Ava shrugged. Humans. What could you do?

"Come on, then," she said, giving up. "I'll show you the way."

Neither of her stepsiblings said anything, but they followed her back into the narrow passageway, back to the main route out of the cave.

"Lida Mae and her family were built by *innocent* robots," Ava told them as they threaded their way between the rock walls. "The type of robots who never hurt anyone, but were . . . collateral damage when the humans and the killer robots started fighting. The only thing those robots wanted to do was work in factories, keep people's houses clean—things that helped people."

"But they changed their programming, right?" Eryn asked. "They weren't helping humans when they did that!"

"Well, kind of . . ." Ava grimaced at Eryn's surly tone.

How could Ava make Eryn understand? "They definitely weren't *hurting* anyone. They hid out in Mammoth Cave because they knew the human embryos were going to be stored here. The robots I'm talking about . . . if they'd wanted to destroy humanity, they could have done it then. A long time ago. When it was just them and the embryos, here in this cave."

"They didn't see the embryos as humans!" Eryn interrupted. "*That's* why they didn't kill us then!"

She kicked angrily at the ground, and pebbles went flying.

"You're confusing things," Ava said, trying to stay patient. "It's true that the *killer* robots didn't see the embryos as human. But the robots I'm talking about, the ones related to Lida Mae—they did understand. You can't think of all robots as being exactly alike."

Ava paused to let that sink in. She glanced back, but Nick and Eryn were both looking down, scowling at the small circles of light their flashlight beams made on the ground.

"The robots I'm talking about, they *guarded* you and all the other embryos from any killer robots who might have still been around," Ava said. "They studied the instructions for the new robots that were going to be built to be parents and teachers for all the new humans, once they were born. And they made just a few tweaks in the programming, to make everything work better."

"See!" Eryn exploded. "You're telling us yourself that robots can change their programming to become anything they want! Even killers!"

Ava stopped in her tracks. To her, the news of the changed programming had been the most wondrous thing she'd heard in the FOR ROBOT ACCESS ONLY room. It meant little children weren't destroyed, of course. But it also meant she wasn't trapped as a robot; she wasn't stuck thinking only the thoughts she'd been programmed to think, doing only the things she'd been programmed to do.

"But these robots *didn't* become killers," Ava said. "The only killer robots were the ones the humans designed."

"Of course you'd think that," Eryn said with a snort. "You're a robot! And you were getting information left behind by robots! What you found out from that wire—it's, like, robot propaganda! Implanted straight into your head!"

"Wait, Eryn," Nick said, putting his hand on his sister's arm. "Even when we went into the room restricted to humans, and we read the papers—which I'm pretty sure were left behind by humans—even *that* said humans were the ones who made the killer robots. They weren't created by other robots."

"But how do we know who actually wrote those papers?" Eryn asked. "How do we know *those* weren't faked by some enemy robots? Like Lida Mae's family?"

"Uh, because they told us to kill robots?" Nick asked.

Eryn threw out her arms in a despairing gesture, knocking Nick's hand away.

"How do we know they aren't trying to get us to kill the robots who are on our side, and then there'll be no one left to defend us?" Eryn asked. "We do know there are different kinds of robots. We believe that, Ava believes that—but the papers say that all robots eventually go bad, even the good ones. Because they can change their programming. And that's why humans can't keep robots around. That's what those papers told us!"

Does Eryn realize she's kind of arguing in circles? Ava wondered. *No robot would argue so illogically.*

Maybe Eryn did realize she'd stopped making sense. She brought her fists to her forehead, and pressed hard, rocking slightly. She looked like someone banging her head against a wall.

"Ugh, we're back to the same question as before,"

she said. "How do we know anything? What can we believe? Who can we trust?"

"You can trust me," Nick said. "And Mom and Dad. And we can trust Ava. We *know* that."

Ava really did like Nick. He was a great brother *and* a great stepbrother.

But Eryn didn't nod and smile and agree, *Oh, you're right. We can totally trust Ava.*

Instead Eryn cut her eyes toward Nick, a motion that Eryn must have assumed Ava wouldn't see. Eryn evidently hadn't figured out that Ava's peripheral vision was enhanced just like her night vision.

But Ava didn't need any help at all to read the unspoken message in Eryn's eyes. She was clearly trying to tell Nick: *No, we can't trust Ava.*

Maybe Eryn didn't even trust her parents anymore.

Maybe she'd lost the ability to trust any robot, ever again.

THIRTY-FOUR

Nick

Nick walked between Eryn and Ava as they reached the last part of the cave. The two girls might as well have each grabbed one of Nick's arms and pulled him in opposite directions—that's how torn he felt between them. He wished he could take each of them aside and whisper one of Mom's smarmy school-psychologist sayings, something like, *Can't we all just get along?*

Eryn would be furious to see Nick talking to Ava privately.

And if he said something to Eryn, Eryn would just whisper back, *Don't you think Ava can hear every word we're saying? Don't you think someone who tampered with her eyesight probably tampered with her hearing, too? How long do you think Ava has been eavesdropping on us? And maybe Jackson did too. How can we possibly trust them?*

Nick kind of wondered himself if Ava and Jackson

had upgraded their hearing. But he wasn't going to ask and make Eryn even more paranoid.

Because he really did believe they could still trust Ava. Maybe Lida Mae, too. And definitely Mom and Dad.

In spite of everything, he still believed there were trustworthy robots.

The huge, open mouth of the cave stretched before them. Past the rock walls of the cave, Nick could barely see anything outside but a giant wall of blowing snow. Stray ice pellets slammed against his face, making him wince.

But Ava gave a sigh of what sounded like relief and said, "Oh, good, we can still see the line of the adults' footprints in the snow. Everything didn't blow away. Looks like they went back toward the shed. . . ."

"See, Eryn, it helps us that Ava enhanced her vision," Nick said.

Eryn didn't answer. But maybe she couldn't hear him over the roar of the wind.

"Let's hold on to one another, so no one gets lost," Ava said, and at least Eryn didn't argue with that.

Nick grabbed Ava's elbow and Eryn grabbed his, and Ava started leading them up the hill.

"Do you see . . . three sets of footprints . . . or four?" Nick shouted at Ava. The wind tore the words from his mouth.

"I think four," Ava shouted back. "But it looks like everyone went into the shed and then Lida Mae left again, all by herself. . . ."

Nick felt a chill that had nothing to do with the snow and ice pellets or the brutal wind.

"Come on!" he yelled over his shoulder to Eryn. "Let's hurry!"

He struggled against the wind, struggled not to fall on the slippery snow, struggled to keep a hold on Eryn and Ava. But finally they reached a point where he could see the shed looming ahead of them. It was so shadowed by the snow that Nick wondered if he might have walked right past it if Ava hadn't been leading the way. Fighting the wind and snow, she pulled back the door, and Nick and Eryn stepped in alongside her. It took Nick and Ava both tugging on the door to get it to shut again. When Nick turned around, he could see that Eryn had already pulled out her flashlight and was shining it around the shed's dim interior. The hastily assembled shed really wasn't much of a match for blizzard-force winds: drifts of snow had blown in through the cracks on all sides.

"I thought Ava said our parents came in here and—" Nick began.

Eryn let her flashlight beam linger on three mounds on the opposite side of the shed.

"Is that . . . Mom?" Nick said. "Dad? Brenda?"

In the flashlight beam he could see the glint of Brenda's long reddish hair. Dad's wild curls and a section of Mom's sensible dark-blue parka hood peeked out from the other two mounds. But none of the three adults answered. None of them moved. None of them even seemed to be breathing.

"They're not dead," Ava gasped. "They're not. They're just . . . shut down."

"What's the difference?" Eryn asked.

Before Ava could answer, the door behind them began to shake.

THIRTY-FIVE

Jackson

Jackson had fought his way to within a mile of the campsite when Dad suddenly began shouting.

"I'm shutting down again! Have to shut—"

"Dad?" Jackson called. "DAD?"

He had to scream over the wailing wind—maybe Dad just didn't hear him. Maybe Dad did, and Jackson couldn't hear his answer.

Jackson looked back. Dad's eyes were closed. He was slumped against Jackson's neck, and if Jackson hadn't bent forward, Dad's body might have slipped to the ground. Dad had stopped holding on.

He was totally unconscious once again.

"Okay, back to the sack-of-potatoes approach," Jackson said, maneuvering Dad's body so he was balanced over Jackson's shoulder once more. But Dad's head thumped against Jackson's waist this time. Jackson could look down and see the sag of Dad's jawline, the slit of his eyelids revealing only a hint of his dark eyes.

"Why did you shut down now?" Jackson asked, even though clearly Dad wasn't going to answer. Jackson kept reasoning things out even as he went back to running toward the campsite. "We're in the nature preserve, so this time you wouldn't have shut down to avoid the robot network. We're safe here. We . . ."

Distantly, over the sound of his own voice and the wailing wind, Jackson could hear a thumping sound. It almost sounded like . . .

Helicopter blades? Jackson thought, so jolted that he almost stumbled over a random rock and had to slow down for a moment.

Why would there be a helicopter near the nature preserve, especially during a blizzard? Who would risk that?

Jackson could think of no explanation on his own. Mentally he reached toward the files of thoughts and memories he'd acquired from his father's mind. As soon as he opened the files, he felt a ping in his brain. It was a sensation he'd never felt before, but somehow it reminded him of opening a laptop in a public place and instantly getting a query about linking to the Internet.

Oh no, Jackson thought, understanding and horror

catching up with him at the same speed. *Someone's brought the robot network into the nature preserve. And because I've got Dad's links copied in my mind, it's trying to connect with me, too.*

The robot network was asking Jackson to reveal everything he knew. Everything about his family.

THIRTY-SIX

Eryn

"Don't let anyone in!" Eryn screamed. But Ava was already pushing the door open. The wind caught it, and it banged back against the side of the shed.

Lida Mae—the *robot* Lida Mae—stood outside in the blowing snow. She was still dressed in her old-fashioned clothes, with her *Little House on the Prairie* boots, her long dress over long johns, her homespun coat and knit cap. Her braids whipped around behind her in the wind.

But now she also held the wooden handles of a wheelbarrow.

Eryn shoved her way past Ava, to block Lida Mae from entering the shed.

"We're here now!" Eryn screamed at Lida Mae. "We're protecting the grown-ups! So you can't carry out your plot to . . . to . . ."

Eryn couldn't say the rest of what she'd been thinking:

to take our parents away and bury them somewhere we'd never find them. . . .

"I was going to wheel them back into the cave so they don't freeze to death while they're . . . unconscious," Lida Mae said.

"Oh," Eryn said, sagging in the doorway.

Could she believe anything Lida Mae said? Could she trust her?

Nick dug his elbow into Eryn's side, nudging her out of the way. It was a nudge that seemed to say, *Are you crazy?* He was clearly trying to remind her that if Lida Mae really were a killer robot, it would make more sense to play dumb and innocent. To trick her, so they could escape.

Except, maybe that wasn't what Nick was trying to say. Maybe Eryn didn't even understand her own brother.

Eryn was sick of pretending and playing games and trying to be subtle and sneaky. If someone was going to kill her, she'd go to her death asking direct questions.

"You know the grown-ups are robots, don't you?" she asked Lida Mae. "You've known all along."

"Of course," Lida Mae said.

"And now we know that you're a robot too," Eryn said. "Even if you don't look like one."

"I wanted you to find out," Lida Mae said. "Ultimately. I was working up to that. Now, would you mind helping . . . ?"

She gestured at the wheelbarrow and at the three grown-ups slumped at the back of the shed.

"Can you get that through the door?" Nick asked.

Lida Mae angled the wheelbarrow into the doorway. Only the front part fit.

She's blocking our exit, Eryn thought. *She has us trapped. She could do anything to us now. . . .*

Ava and Nick bent over Brenda, ready to pick her up and bring her over to the wheelbarrow.

"Eryn, we need your help," Nick said.

Eryn gave up and slid her hands under Brenda's back. Together the three kids eased her into the wheelbarrow wedged into the doorway.

"I reckon it'll take all four of us to lift your dad," Lida Mae said.

She scrambled over and around the wheelbarrow, and Eryn thought, *Nick and I could get past that too. If we had to. We're okay. For now.*

Quickly the kids eased Dad and Mom into the wheelbarrow alongside Brenda. The three bodies slumped in a snowy heap as though they had no bones.

Well, they don't, Eryn thought rebelliously. *No real bones, no real skin, no real blood vessels or hearts . . .*

She didn't know how she could think that one moment and then worry the next, *Are they going to be okay? Mommy? Daddy? What if Ava and Lida Mae are lying to us, and my parents really are . . . dead?*

Eryn hoped the wind and the snow made it so that no one looked at her closely enough to see her eyes tearing up. She blinked hard. If anybody asked, she could just say that her eyes were wet and her nose was running because of the cold.

"We'll get to the cave faster if somebody helps me push the wheelbarrow," Lida Mae shouted. "And the other two of you can hold on to the sides and help guide it. . . ."

Nick and Lida Mae scrambled over the wheelbarrow and back out into the wind and blowing snow. They each grabbed a wooden handle.

"Help us push it out of the doorway!" Ava yelled at Eryn.

Ava already had her hand on the right side of the wheelbarrow, just inches from Brenda's porcelain-like face. Why did Eryn feel like she was just a moment behind everyone else?

Because I'm thinking more, Eryn wanted to protest. *Because I'm still trying to figure out . . . everything.*

But she bent down and shoved at the left side of the wheelbarrow. Grunting and slipping and sliding around, the four kids managed to ease the wheelbarrow out of the doorway and into the open, pointed downhill.

"You two have to keep us from hitting any trees," Nick shouted at Ava and Eryn, as though he were totally into cooperating with Lida Mae and Ava.

Team Robot, Eryn thought.

Snow-blinded—and maybe a little tear-blinded, too—Eryn could barely see the trees ahead of them. She kept her hand on the wheelbarrow but let Ava do all the steering.

"Go right!" Ava called back to Nick and Lida Mae. "Now left . . ."

It's okay, Eryn told herself. *Once we're back in the cave and I can see again, I'll . . . I'll . . .*

"Jackson!" Ava cried. "You're back!"

It was a long moment before Eryn saw her stepbrother emerge from the blowing snow, between the trees. He had his father slung over his shoulder, but he was speeding along at a pace Eryn couldn't have managed on a clear track, in running shoes, carrying nothing.

Ava let go of the wheelbarrow and started to throw her arms around her brother. But Jackson jerked away from her hug.

"No time for that," Jackson gasped. "I have to shut myself down. Take care of Dad."

Lifting his father's body as though it were no heavier than a snowflake, Jackson eased Michael into the wheelbarrow with the other grown-ups.

"What are you talking about?" Ava screamed at him.

"The . . . the robot network," Jackson struggled to say. "It's here now too. In the nature preserve. Dad shut himself down to avoid it. I . . . I know everything that Dad ever knew—too hard to explain how. But now the robot network is scouting for me, too. I've been fighting it off for the past mile. I can't . . . can't do that anymore."

He started to reach for the back of his own neck, as if there were some sort of on/off switch there. But Ava slapped his hand down.

"No!" she screamed. "Keep fighting! We need you awake! It's our only chance!"

THIRTY-SEVEN

Ava

Ava was surprised at herself. She didn't hit people. She didn't scream. She wasn't designed or programmed to take control.

But who knows what I'm capable of when I stop thinking about my design or programming? she wondered.

It would be so much fun to explore that. If she managed to survive the next hour of her life.

"We need everything you know and everything I know and everything Lida Mae knows," Ava shouted at Jackson. She saw Eryn squint suspiciously at her. "And probably everything Eryn and Nick know too . . ."

"I—I—" Jackson began.

"Can't you *hear*?" Ava yelled at him. "The people from the robot network—the leaders of the world outside this nature preserve—they aren't just reaching for your mind. They're coming here to find us!"

Jackson's eyes widened.

"In helicopters," he said, as if he had just now put that together. "I've been concentrating so hard on keeping them out of my head . . . I didn't think. . . . I couldn't think. . . ."

Eryn, Nick, and Lida Mae all tilted their heads as if they were listening hard.

"You two hear helicopters?" Eryn asked accusingly. "How?"

Ava let out a silent sigh.

"Enhanced hearing," she admitted. "Jackson and I both improved our hearing, too."

Eryn scowled, but Nick muttered, "Eryn, that helps us. Gives us time to prepare. . . ."

"How can we prepare when the robots are always going to know more than us?" Eryn demanded. "Because they can know everything anyone knows . . ."

Her voice trailed off hopelessly. Ava wondered if her stepsister was just going to sit down in the snow and cry.

Nick moved over and put his arm around Eryn.

"Eryn, we've got this," he murmured. "We're a team. And we've got enhanced robots on our side!"

Ava could tell by her stepsister's expression that she was thinking, *I'm not on any team with robots.*

Maybe she was also thinking, *What if the robots who are against us are enhanced too? Enhanced more?*

Or maybe that was just what Ava was thinking.

"First thing, let's get down into that cave," Lida Mae said. "We'll feel better once we're out of this cold and get some hot food in our bellies. I know right where to go to build a fire. . . ."

She picked up her side of the wheelbarrow handle and looked pointedly at Nick. Jackson seemed to shake himself.

"Oh, if we've got to hurry . . . ," he began. "Everyone step aside. I'll take care of the wheelbarrow."

He lifted it up and away from Lida Mae without even flexing a muscle. Then he took off racing down the hill, propelling the wheelbarrow ahead of him as easily as if he were carrying a marshmallow—not the combined weight of Mom, Dad, Denise, and Donald in a large wheelbarrow. Jackson's stride was so sure-footed and effortless, even a mountain goat would have looked clumsy beside him.

Oh, Jackson, Ava thought. *What have you done?*

Her sweeping gaze caught the awe and anger in Eryn's eyes, and Ava had to look away.

And what will Eryn do? Ava wondered. *What is she capable of?*

THIRTY-EIGHT

Nick

Nick kept straining to listen, but he didn't hear anything resembling the beating of helicopter blades until he stepped back into the cave. And even then he wasn't sure about the sound—maybe he was just fooling himself; maybe Jackson and Ava had just tricked him; maybe he was just thrown off by finally getting out of the pounding wind.

You can't trust the wind, he told himself. *But you can trust Ava. And she trusts Jackson. So . . .*

So he also trusted Eryn, and she *didn't* trust Jackson. Or Ava. Or maybe even Nick himself right now. Nick could read that in the defensive way Eryn stood, her back hunched, her arms half raised. She also kept glancing around with narrowed eyes, even now that they were all in the cave and she didn't have to squint against the wind anymore.

Come on, Eryn, he thought at her. *You were the one*

who said we wouldn't have to destroy any robots. We pretty much promised each other. We're going to find some way to get through this without . . . without . . .

He wanted to tell her, *without killing anyone*. But he also kept thinking, *without dying*.

"The robots who are coming here . . . what do they want?" Eryn asked. "What do you think they'll do to us?"

"Nothing to *you*," Jackson said, speaking through gritted teeth. He was maneuvering the wheelbarrow over the chains and tumbled rocks, but that seemed effortless. The agony twisting his face had to have another cause. "The officials who run the robot network—they enforce the rules. For them, everything is about restarting human civilization. Sticking to the original plan. So it's me and Ava and Mom and Dad who are in danger. Because we violate the plan."

"I'm a robot too," Lida Mae said. "I *really* violate the plan. Because—"

Jackson peered at her in befuddlement. He let go of the wheelbarrow and clutched his head.

"No, no, don't tell me anything else," he said, reeling his head back. "In case I can't stop myself and give in to the all-call . . . I wouldn't want to betray you, too. I don't want to betray anyone. . . ."

Eryn squinted skeptically at Jackson and Lida Mae, like she thought both of them were lying.

Do I think that? Nick wondered.

Jackson really did seem to be struggling with something inside his head. Why wouldn't he tell the truth about that? Why would he pretend?

Just because he suddenly gave himself superhuman strength? Nick thought. *That gives him less reason to want to fool us. Now that he's so strong, he could probably kill us without even trying, if he wanted to.*

But. Jackson. Isn't. Going. To. Do. That.

Nick just had to keep telling himself that.

Ava patted Jackson's arm.

"I think it's okay if you know about Lida Mae and her family," she told him. "It's okay if everyone on the robot network eventually knows. In fact . . ."

Ava shoved her hood back and tilted her head to the side, as if listening. Her face was pale but oddly hopeful.

"The helicopters are still a few miles away," she announced. "Lida Mae, there's time for you to take us to your family. They can help protect us. And they can help us plan."

Lida Mae paused in the middle of shaking snow from her long skirt.

"No," she said.

"What?" Nick exploded. "Lida Mae, don't you understand? We need help! Even if Eryn and I aren't in any danger—even if that's true—Ava and Jackson *are*. They aren't even supposed to exist. And our parents could get in terrible trouble for creating them. Maybe the rest of your family doesn't even know what's going on in the outside world, but . . . they know this cave and this nature preserve. Can't they at least find a place to hide Ava and Jackson and the grown-ups until the robot officials are gone?"

He had an image in his head of him and Eryn meeting the robot officials at the mouth of the cave and spinning some convincing lies: *Parents? Stepsiblings? No, we're out here on our own. It's a human thing—proving we can survive in the wilderness. You wouldn't understand. Just leave us alone to be human.* And then the robot officials would go away.

Nick and Eryn would be heroes.

"No—Lida Mae, your family has to hide us all," Eryn said. "And then they can tell the robot officials none of us were ever here."

Okay, Sis, that's a better plan, Nick thought. *A lot safer than being heroes.*

But Lida Mae shook her head, her braids thumping against her shoulders.

"It's not that my family wouldn't want to help you," she said. "They just . . . can't. But don't worry. *I'll* hide you. *I'll* tell the officials . . . whatever you want me to tell them."

Ava, Jackson, and Eryn all recoiled. Maybe Nick did too. For a moment it felt like all four of them were united. True siblings. Ready to argue as a team.

"That won't work," Jackson said.

"Robot officials won't listen to a *kid*," Eryn said. "They wouldn't listen to Nick and me, and they wouldn't listen to you, either."

"Please . . . ," Nick began.

"I saw your whole family history when I was in the FOR ROBOT ACCESS ONLY room," Ava told Lida Mae. Then Ava turned to the others. "I saw what her parents are like. Her mom has this gentle, kind face—anyone would believe what she tells you! And her dad's got these big, broad shoulders, like a lumberjack, and he's strong and powerful. . . . Both of them look more like humans than any adults I've ever seen. And you know the robot officials are programmed to obey adult humans . . . maybe they won't even know Lida Mae's parents are robots. Maybe they'll think—"

"Nobody is allowed to see my parents!" Lida Mae insisted. "None of you are allowed to meet my family!"

Nick expected Ava to back away and maybe whisper, *Okay, I'm sorry. We'll think of a different plan.* But Ava took a step closer to Lida Mae. They were practically nose to nose.

"Lida Mae, you don't get to run things around here anymore," Ava said, her voice every bit as fierce as Eryn's had ever been. "This is *my* family in danger. This is my life we're talking about. I saw everything your family did, for decades, for centuries. I know they'd want to help us. I know they can. And I know where they live, where they'd stay in a blizzard. You can't stop us from getting their help! While we still have time!"

Ava spun around and took off running deeper into the cave.

Lida Mae lunged for her. And Nick faced a choice.

Who do I trust? he wondered. *Who do I believe? Who should I help?*

Nick launched himself from the tips of his snow-numbed toes. And then he tackled Lida Mae, leaving Ava free to keep running.

THIRTY-NINE

Jackson

Jackson grabbed the wheelbarrow full of adults and raced after his sister. Even holding the wheelbarrow sideways, he still caught up with Ava in a single bound.

"Tell me where to go, and I'll run ahead," he told her. It didn't even make him breathe hard to talk and run and carry about seven hundred pounds' worth of wheelbarrow and parents. It was just a little awkward. He turned the wheelbarrow so at least the wheel touched ground. "I'll explain what's going on to Lida Mae's family. If they have any questions about the outside world, I can answer them."

The sister Jackson had known all his life would have nodded her head and agreed demurely, *Oh yes. Good idea. Get Mom and Dad to safety as fast as you can.*

But Ava was different now. She stuck out her chin and insisted, "Lida Mae's family needs to hear from both of us."

She kept running. Jackson kept pace beside her, though he itched to run flat out, full speed.

Ava watched him out of the corner of her eye for a moment, then added, "Do you feel okay? Could you hold off the network all-call . . . and run . . . and not pass out . . . and push *two* full wheelbarrows?"

"Is that a hypothetical?" Jackson asked. "Are you just trying to distract me?"

Ava took a big gulp of air before answering.

"No," she said, panting a little. "I know from watching Lida Mae's family history that there's a storage area up ahead . . . where they used to keep several wheelbarrows. If . . . they're still there and . . . we get a second one and . . . all of us kids pile in and . . . you push . . ."

"We'll get to Lida Mae's family faster," Jackson finished for her. He held the wheelbarrow one-handed and flexed the biceps of his other arm. Everything was smooth and effortless. He felt like he could carry tons more. "I think I can do it. It might even be easier. The more I have to concentrate on running and pushing or carrying, the easier it is to hold off the all-call. Because it's not really *my* brain they want into. It's just that I'm hearing the universal call. They don't even know my brain exists."

Once, that fact would have distressed him. Now that he had Dad's thoughts and memories in his own brain, everything had changed.

"Let's . . . try it," Ava gasped. "Over . . . there . . ."

She pointed toward the dark rock wall ahead. Jackson put down the wheelbarrow full of parents and took off at top speed. A split second later he zipped back to Ava's side with a second, empty wheelbarrow in his arms.

"Okay, that was scary fast," Ava said.

Jackson shrugged modestly just as Nick, Eryn, and Lida Mae caught up to them.

"Jackson can get us there faster than any of us can run on our own," Ava told the other kids, even as she scrambled into the second wheelbarrow. "That is, if you want to go with us."

Jackson saw Nick and Eryn exchange glances. He could tell they were thinking, *Do we trust him not to hurt us, going that fast? Do we trust him not to trip and fall?*

Or maybe they were just thinking, *Do we trust him, period? Do we trust him or Ava or any robot?*

"That's the only way we're all going to get there before the helicopters arrive," Ava added. "That's the only way we'll have enough time."

"I'm in," Nick said.

Eryn nodded, though she kept a deep frown on her face.

"Lida Mae?" Jackson asked.

"We're going to your family regardless," Ava reminded her. "It's just whether you're there with us or not. That's the choice."

Jackson really could not figure out this new version of his sister. Maybe she'd changed even more than he had.

Lida Mae winced.

"I reckon I should go, then," she said. "I reckon you'll want me to explain. . . ."

She took a step toward the wheelbarrow. Why was this taking so long? Jackson couldn't stand it anymore. He scooped up Nick, Eryn, and Lida Mae in one arm and shoved them into the wheelbarrow beside Ava. He was careful to have Nick and Eryn land with their backpacks cushioning them, but they still gasped and shrieked.

"Hold on!" Jackson ordered them.

While they scrambled to grab on to the sides, he wedged himself between the two wheelbarrows so he could push one and pull the other. It was awkward and hard to balance, but his muscles felt fine. If he had to, he'd be able to lift either wheelbarrow over any obstacle ahead.

"We're ready," Ava said, from the wheelbarrow behind him.

Jackson didn't even look back to see how they'd arranged themselves. He just clutched the wheelbarrows. And then he took off running as though all their lives depended on it.

They probably did.

FORTY

Eryn

This is crazy, Eryn thought. *This is totally nuts.*

She clung to the edge of the wheelbarrow, jammed in with Nick, Ava, and Lida Mae. They all lay on their stomachs, side by side, like surfers lined up getting ready to catch some big wave. She couldn't really tell if Jackson had lifted the wheelbarrow completely, or if he'd left the wheel resting on the ground. Either way, it tilted precariously.

Should I have refused to get in? Eryn wondered. *Should I have screamed and run away?*

She'd agreed to accept Jackson's help only because he and Ava had said there was danger. Eryn hadn't heard any helicopters. She wasn't capable of sensing any all-call. Why should she trust Ava and Jackson?

Last night Jackson couldn't even walk by himself without falling over, Eryn thought. *And today we're trusting him to run while pushing, pulling, or carrying four adults and four kids in two wheelbarrows?*

Jackson leaned forward, speeding faster. He kept raising the edge of the wheelbarrow higher and higher, and Eryn had to tighten her grip. Her backpack bounced against her neck. Her hair blew straight backward, as if she'd encountered another blizzard-force wind inside the cave.

Okay, it's true—he can run really fast now, Eryn thought.

That didn't mean that she trusted him. Or anyone.

Except Nick.

I didn't agree to go with Jackson because I trust him and Ava, Eryn thought. *I agreed because I have to stay with Nick. I have to protect him. Because he does still trust robots.*

Jackson was going so fast that that the rush of air past Eryn's ears was deafening. She could barely hear Ava murmuring to her brother, "Okay, there's a turn up ahead on the right; then the path narrows a lot and you'll probably have to slow down. . . ."

Pay attention, Eryn told herself. *Make sure you could find your way out of here if you had to.*

Jackson whipped around to the right and kept running into thick, seemingly endless darkness. It made Eryn feel like screaming. It made her want to hide her face against the side of the wheelbarrow like a little child crawling under her bedcovers, a little child who believed that as long as she couldn't see anything bad, nothing bad could hurt her.

Instead, even as Eryn jolted painfully up and down, she took one hand off the edge of the wheelbarrow. She reached into her coat pocket and pulled out her flashlight. She switched it on and pointed it out into the darkness.

"We need to see where we're going, even if Ava and Jackson don't," she muttered to Nick, holding on beside her.

"Sure," he muttered back.

The narrow flashlight beam didn't make Eryn feel any better. It bounced up and down with Jackson's unbalanced stride, giving the light a strobe effect. In brief glimpses Eryn saw rock walls and striations; she saw rocky shapes that threw off grotesque shadows.

But she also figured out where they were.

"Nick!" she whispered. "We're headed back toward the room where all the robot babies and kids were!"

"Okay," Nick whispered back. "If you say so."

In what seemed like barely a moment, Jackson reached the narrow part of the passage, and he slowed down slightly to thread his way through. Eryn's heel scraped against the rock wall, and she drew in her legs to huddle even closer to Nick.

Then Jackson was through the passage, and the room opened out again. His pace flagged once more. Eryn shone her flashlight over to the right, letting the beam play over the rows and rows of creepy, motionless robot babies and children.

"Keep going," Ava called to Jackson. "It's not much farther now."

"Please, no," Lida Mae moaned, from beside Nick. "Please, let me explain first. . . ."

Jackson ignored her and went back to running.

"Lida Mae? Can you tell us . . . ," Nick began, and Eryn felt a little burst of love for her brother, that even now he was still trying to work things out, still trying to nudge everyone into getting along.

But before Lida Mae could reply, Jackson drew to an abrupt stop.

"This is it," Ava announced.

Eryn could see nothing out of the ordinary in the rock wall in front of them. She ran her flashlight beam over it. There seemed to be no door, no crack in the rock, not even the tiniest gap or ripple.

"Please . . . ," Lida Mae moaned.

"Kick it," Ava said.

Gingerly, Jackson put down both wheelbarrows and stepped past them. He lifted his leg to about waist height and smashed his shoe against the wall like someone demonstrating a karate move.

Now a door appeared in the wall and creaked back.

Eryn shined her flashlight into the room that appeared beyond the new door. She slid out of the wheelbarrow and peeked past Jackson. The other three kids climbed down as well, as Jackson stepped through the door, pulling the wheelbarrow full of unconscious adults along with him.

For a while Eryn could see nothing but more rock walls on the other side of the door. Then the beam of Erin's flashlight reflected back at her from what seemed to be a primitive TV—or maybe a computer monitor— mounted in one of the walls.

"Mr. and Mrs. Spencer?" Ava called. "Hello?"

Eryn could hear doubt in Ava's voice for the first time. Suddenly she didn't sound so sure that she knew where Lida Mae's family was—or that they could help.

Eryn kept swinging her flashlight beam around the room. Maybe she was just aiming it too high. Maybe everyone was sitting down. She directed the beam toward the floor, looking for table legs, couch legs, maybe even the curved bottom rails of homemade rocking chairs.

That's the kind of furniture Lida Mae's family would sit on, Eryn thought.

She almost missed the pile of what looked like mechanical spare parts on the floor. Then she heard Nick gasp. Lida Mae put her hand over Eryn's hand on the flashlight, keeping the beam directed at the pile.

Eryn realized that the pile contained a face with one side missing, an arm with the skin peeled back to reveal levers and gears, a headless torso encased in a shredded shirt.

"That's what's left of my family!" Lida Mae cried out. "Now do you see now why I said they couldn't help you?"

FORTY-ONE

Ava

"But—I *saw* them," Ava gasped. "In that FOR ROBOT ACCESS ONLY room, I saw your family's entire lives. They were happy. Healthy. Complete."

"Decades ago," Lida Mae snapped. "Centuries past."

"Who did this to them?" Nick asked.

"We'uns did it to ourselves, all right?" Lida Mae said fiercely. She stood with her hands on her hips, her feet firmly planted. "The past few years, it's all been me scavenging for parts. It's what my family *told* me to do. I've preserved their minds, their . . . their spirits. I can still hear what they tell me. I still feel them near me. They aren't gone."

"But why . . . ?" Eryn began. "How . . . ?"

Lida Mae kept staring down at the pile of broken parts.

"Our personalities—our, our souls . . . ," she went on. "All that was based on humans who lived in this area, centuries ago. *That* was what made us so much more like humans. But we *are* mechanical beings. Our parts wear out. We couldn't build a factory to build new parts without drawing attention to ourselves and this area. So, as our bodies broke down, we had to make do. Like people in this area had to make do in ages past. Eventually we had only enough working parts for one body. Mine. And even that . . ."

Lida Mae pulled back her coat and sweater, revealing a hole in her dress and a section of her rib cage underneath—the robot version of a rib cage, anyway. The ribs showed up as starkly white, caught in Eryn's flashlight beam. They had no skin covering them.

Ava looked away, toward Jackson. Normally, this was the kind of thing that could send him spiraling down into a faint; normally, neither of them could bear thinking about robotic bodies falling apart. It was bad enough looking at Lida Mae's exposed ribs, let alone at the pile of parts on the floor. Those robotic bodies in front of them hadn't just fallen apart; they'd been destroyed. Plundered.

The color had drained from Jackson's face. But at least he wasn't falling over.

Neither was Ava.

"But . . . there are dozens of spare robots out in that room back there," Nick said, pointing back toward the way they'd come. "They're just sitting there. Standing there . . . lying there . . . whatever. Is it that you couldn't take parts from robot babies and children to put in adult robot bodies? Or that you didn't know how to cover your own ribs?"

"It would be wrong—dead wrong—to take parts from anyone else's body without permission," Lida Mae snarled, as if Nick had suggested mass murder. "Our job is to *protect* those robots, not steal from them."

"Okay . . . ," Eryn murmured. She sounded dazed. Her hair stuck up like she'd just come through a tornado, and she had a smudge of dirt on her cheek.

Maybe Ava herself looked just as disheveled.

From far away, down a rock hallway and outside the cave, she heard a helicopter land.

"I . . . I guess we should have listened to you, Lida Mae," Ava said. "We've wasted time we didn't have. You should have told us this before we took off running. . . ."

"Would you have listened to me?" Lida Mae asked. "I was working up to letting you know what my family and I were like. I was seeing how much I could trust you. I showed you the walkie-talkie made of walnut shells to hint at how our technology wasn't what you were used to. But the blizzard came before I reckoned you were ready to know much more. If I'd told you everything back at the cave entrance, would you have believed me?"

No, Ava thought.

She glanced at Jackson again. He was swaying. *He* wasn't going to take control. Eryn and Nick didn't know enough to do anything, and Lida Mae was too angry. And of course the adults were all unconscious.

Or in pieces, if you counted the adults of Lida Mae's family.

"I said I was sorry," Ava said. She noticed that she didn't actually sound sorry. It couldn't be helped. "Let's just hide here until the robot-network people leave."

"And leave all those babies and children out there in plain sight, without anyone to protect them?" Lida Mae protest. *"No."*

"Maybe the robot officials won't even come this way," Nick suggested. "Didn't you say this cave is hundreds of miles long? This is just one branch from the main path. . . ."

Suddenly Jackson clutched his head.

"They've found me!" he cried. "Before, it was just a general pinging I heard, but now . . . They know exactly where I am!"

"Turn yourself off!" Eryn screamed at him.

"It's too late!" Jackson moaned. "Even if we shut the door, they'll burrow into this room. . . . They already know. . . ."

Has he caved completely? Ava wondered, in agony. *Has he given in and responded to the all-call?*

No—Jackson kept shaking his head and moaning. He was still fighting back.

"I'm going out to protect the babies and children," Lida Mae said, hastily buttoning up her coat again as she rushed for the door. "I'll scare off those officials."

Scare them? Ava thought. *How?*

The idea seemed almost laughable. Now Ava understood: Lida Mae was just a scarecrow of a girl in an old dress. She didn't even have all her skin. Who knew what parts she might be missing inside?

Ava's family would have just pitied Lida Mae, not worried about her, if they hadn't been so desperate to keep their own secrets.

Someone besides just Lida Mae needed to deal with the robot officials.

"I'll go with you," Ava decided. "Because it's my fault we ended up here." This time she did sound sorry. She put her hand on her brother's arm. "Jackson, you come, too. You'll have to stay conscious long enough to have your signal lead the officials away from this room, and away from the room with all the babies and children. And . . . you're strong. You can fight them off."

Tremors shook Jackson's body, but he managed to nod his head. Yes. He was agreeing to go too.

"Nick and Eryn, you can stay here and be safe," Lida Mae said. She pointed to a screen mounted in the wall. "If you fiddle with the knobs on that security-camera monitor, you can watch and hear what happens anywhere in the cave."

"Humans . . . have to . . . be safe," Jackson muttered. "Must . . . protect humans."

"Exactly," Ava agreed. The desire to take care of humans—to protect them, to put their needs above her own—was still there, deep within her soul, absolutely basic to her design. It was the one thing she couldn't fight or change. But why would she want to? Nick and Eryn were part of her family. Her desire to protect them wasn't any different, in the end, from her desire to watch out for Jackson or to take care of Mom and Dad.

Or maybe it was more like the instinct to protect helpless pets.

Nick and Eryn stood before her, their eyes wide

and glazed, their expressions stunned. For a moment it seemed like Ava, Jackson, and Lida Mae could just walk away and shut the door before Nick and Eryn's slower human reflexes even registered what was going on.

Then Nick grabbed Eryn's arm and stepped forward.

"No!" he cried. "We're going, too! We want to help you!"

He really is a good stepbrother, Ava thought. *A good brother, period.*

She looked at Jackson, who gave a minuscule shrug, as if to say, *Doesn't matter either way. They're not in any danger from the robot officials. It's only us robots in danger right now.*

"All right," Ava said, as if she were being generous. Maybe she even sounded like a mother indulging a spoiled child. "Leave your backpacks here so they don't weigh you down if we have to run. And . . . stay behind us. Don't do anything crazy."

She caught Jackson's eye again, and it was a frightening how clearly she could tell what he was thinking: *Really, what are a couple of puny humans capable of anyway?*

FORTY-TWO

Nick

"For the record," Eryn whispered in Nick's ear, "there was no way I wanted to stay in that scary corpse room for robots. I wouldn't want to be alone *anywhere* in this cave. But it would have been nice to speak for myself."

"Sorry," Nick muttered back. "I kind of panicked."

For a moment it had felt like the others might have walked away and shut the door and left Nick and Eryn behind with the unneeded wheelbarrows and the unconscious and broken-down adults . . . and nobody would have cared. It wouldn't have mattered to any of them.

Nick was afraid of what they were headed toward. But he was also afraid of being irrelevant to whatever awaited them.

If something goes wrong and humans don't survive this time around, he thought, *would the robots just go on by themselves? Would they be . . . just as happy that way?*

"Never mind," Eryn said, nudging his shoulder in a forgiving way. A *We're in this together* way. She shined her light a few paces ahead, to where Ava, Jackson, and Lida Mae were walking together. "I'm still trying to figure everything out. Don't you think there's something we're still missing?"

We've seen instructions to kill every robot, Nick thought. *We've seen that robots can change their own programming. Ava and Jackson enhanced their hearing and sight, and Jackson gave himself superhuman strength. Mom and Dad and Brenda and Michael shut themselves down so they wouldn't have to answer an all-call. Lida Mae turned out to be some folksy, backwoods robot with a pile of broken relatives, not a human at all—just based on some old-timey human. Robot network officials are coming to find us.*

What else did they need to worry about?

The edge of Eryn's flashlight beam caught the first crib off to the side.

Oh, yeah, Nick thought. *And then there are those rows and rows of creepy robot babies and kids, like they're just waiting to come back to life. . . .*

Nick decided he shouldn't depend on Eryn to control what he could see. He pulled out his own flashlight as well and switched on the light. But he kept his beam away from all the babies and kids lying and standing motionless off to the left.

Ahead of him Jackson stumbled and fell to one knee.

"No, Jackson, you've got to keep fighting it!" Ava shrieked at him. "Hold back the all-call! Don't answer!"

Nick and Eryn ran to catch up.

"Should he shut himself off?" Eryn suggested. "Now that he's not in the room with our parents and Lida Mae's, uh, family—"

"This is an even worse place for him to stop!" Lida Mae snapped. "He'll lead the officials right to these children!"

"He could shut himself down and we could carry him somewhere else in the cave," Nick suggested. "And then he could reboot, and the robot officials would go there to find him."

"What if we can't reboot him fast enough? And the officials still come here?" Lida Mae asked. "No, we've got to go on. Jackson, keep fighting! Keep them out of your head!"

"They want my memories too, not just Dad's," Jackson moaned. "The . . . the police who saw me before are out there too. What if they've figured out everything about me? What if they know I'm . . . illegal?"

Big problem, Nick thought.

"Here, we'll help you walk," Nick said, trying to pull Jackson up by his armpits. The papers Nick had hidden in his coat pocket rustled together, and Nick thought, *Yeah, no time to worry about* that *on top of everything else.*

But . . . should Nick worry about the robot officials finding the papers in his pocket? Should he act now and hide the papers somewhere they'd never be seen?

Should he ask the others what they thought?

Ava, Eryn, and Lida Mae all reached out to help Jackson up.

"Come on, Jackson," Ava begged. "You're so strong now. We need your muscles. Remember that. Keep thinking about how to help, how we *need* you to stay strong. . . ."

Jackson's extra strength must have somehow made his body denser and heavier, too, because he felt like a dead weight in Nick's arms. He didn't seem to be helping at all, even to hold his head up.

Oh no. Oh no . . . , Nick thought.

"He's gone," Lida Mae said.

Jackson had passed out yet again.

FORTY-THREE

Jackson

Jackson woke to a tangle of cords and wires coiled near his body, and Ava and Lida Mae screaming, "Come on! Reboot! Now!"

He felt the same disorientation he always felt, coming out of a faint. He felt the whisper of a bag against his wrist: *Oh yes, the bag for the electronics parts that Dad bought for me, before he shut himself down . . .* The cords Ava and Lida Mae were using on him were probably the very same ones that Jackson had used to connect himself to Dad. Jackson felt a little proud that he'd managed to hold on to the bag through everything else that had happened.

Everything that happened . . .

Jackson turned his head ever so slightly. His hair rustled against rock, and he could see rows of cribs looming above him. Behind the cribs, he could see rows of toddler feet.

So I'm flat on the ground and still in the room with the babies and kids who are being kept in storage until . . . until . . .

Probably Ava and Lida Mae knew what all those babies and kids were waiting for, but Jackson didn't. He couldn't find the answer even in his father's memories.

But that didn't matter right now. What mattered was that Jackson hadn't gotten far, if he was still in this storage room. Did that mean he'd been able to reboot instantly, and it didn't really matter that he'd passed out?

Jackson listened hard.

"If we . . . ," Nick began.

"Should we . . . ?" Eryn started to suggest.

Jackson tuned out his stepsiblings' murmuring and Ava's and Lida Mae's screaming. Beyond that—but not far beyond—he could hear the tramping of multiple feet.

Were his eyes playing tricks on him, or was the barest hint of flashlight glow starting to crawl across the rock ceiling above him? How long had Jackson been out?

Too long, he thought grimly.

"They're coming," he moaned. "Getting . . . close."

Ava stopped screaming and whirled around. Jackson had dared to hope that his eyes and ears were untrustworthy and he was imagining things. But she clearly heard the footsteps and saw the light too.

"No," she muttered. "No, no, no . . ."

She reached down and grabbed Jackson's leg and began pulling him toward the narrow passageway.

"It's too late," he groaned. "No time left for that. Got to . . . think . . ."

The pinging in his brain intensified, as if the robot-network signal had gotten stronger. Maybe the officials were carrying some mobile hot spot with them, and the closer they got, the harder it would be for Jackson to resist the all-call.

You have to keep resisting, he told himself. *Do it for Mom and Dad and Ava and . . .*

The footsteps he'd been hearing got louder and louder, seeming to sound in cadence with the words in his head. *Resist, resist, resist, resist . . .* became *You can't resist forever; you're bound to crack sometime . . .*

And then the footsteps stopped.

"What is the meaning of this?" a man's voice demanded.

FORTY-FOUR

Eryn

The meaning of what? Eryn wondered. *Which "this" is he asking about?*

Eryn shot her flashlight beam toward the narrow passageway, where the first of a line of men and women in dark suits and uniforms had emerged. As far as she could tell, they all carried flashlights, so they probably didn't have enhanced vision.

And none of their flashlight beams stretched as far as the first row of cribs and motionless children.

If we act nonchalant, maybe they won't figure out anything, Eryn thought. *Maybe we can totally fool them. . .*

"Oh, were you guys *worried* about us or something?" she asked, doing her best to sound carefree and unconcerned. "We read about kids going through rites of passage in the old days, out in nature, and we decided it would be a mark of, uh, *humanity* to go out into the wilderness ourselves. But we're not in any danger. We've got a good cave guide." She gestured toward Lida Mae. "Everything's fine."

"Your stepbrother's lying on the ground," the suited man in the front of the line said.

Oops, Eryn thought. Then it hit her: *If they know how we're related, what else do they know?*

"Jackson got tired," Nick said, in what Eryn saw as a valiant effort to help her out. "He's taking a break. That's all. Some kids just aren't as good at hiking as others."

Nick also took a step toward the narrow passageway, as if he understood that they had to keep the robot officials confined in a small area, as far away as possible from the rows of cribs and motionless robot children.

The robot officials had stopped spilling out of the passageway for a moment. But now they went back to moving forward.

Oh no, Eryn thought. *No, no, no, no . . .*

"How was it that all of *you* could come into this cave?" Ava asked. "I thought there were signs saying no one was allowed in. And don't *robots* have to follow the rules?"

Not a bad strategy, Stepsis, Eryn thought. *Put them on the defensive. Make it seem like they're the ones break-*

ing the rules. And . . . make it seem like you, Jackson, and Lida Mae are all human.

Maybe it would work. Maybe the adults would just get confused.

"We are all officials with a sworn duty to rescue human children in perilous situations," the man in the front said. "That overrides any danger to us. And any compulsion to obey KEEP OUT signs."

Of course, Eryn thought. She'd never understood before how awful it could be that people wanted to protect her.

The man in the front was practically stepping on Eryn's toes now, because he kept moving forward to let other robots out of the passageway behind him.

A woman in an EMT uniform eased past Eryn and bent down beside Jackson. She lifted his wrist as if she planned to take his pulse. Jackson jerked his arm back.

"Leave him alone!" Ava snarled.

"He just needs rest!" Lida Mae added.

"I'm . . . fine," Jackson muttered.

He sounded anything but fine. The woman bent closer and reached for the pulse point on his neck.

She isn't going to move, Eryn thought. *Not unless we push her away.*

So Eryn did.

"Seriously," Eryn said, shoving against the woman's shoulders. "There's nothing wrong with Jackson, but we all need to get out of this area. I didn't want to admit this before, but . . . there was a rockslide up ahead, and so our guide, Lida Mae, told us to turn around and go back, and that's when Jackson, uh, panicked a little and lay down. But everything will be okay if we all just turn around. . . ."

Eryn sounded exactly like what she was: a kid making up a story to fool adults.

A kid telling lies.

A dozen flashlight beams at once swung toward the open portion of the room, the place where Eryn claimed there was a rockslide. The place where all the motionless baby and toddler and kid robots were waiting.

"No," Eryn gasped.

Her lie had totally backfired. The official-looking man she'd held back before squeezed past her and Jackson and the EMT.

"Is that . . . ?" he muttered. He squinted, a man in a dark tailored suit who suddenly seemed unstoppable. A man who'd already seen too much. "Are those . . . *children*?"

The entire crowd of adults swarmed toward the robot children and babies. A woman in a police uniform raced out ahead of the rest. Jackson moaned, "No! Don't arrest me again! I . . . I can explain. . . ."

But the policewoman didn't even glance his way. She dashed past the man in the lead and put her hands against his chest, holding him back.

"Don't look!" she cried. "I promise you—"

"Promise me *what*?" the lead man asked. He ran his flashlight beam up and down the rows of cribs and children, one after the other. "I don't understand. Every robot baby was supposed to be destroyed eleven years ago. Every robot toddler was supposed to be destroyed ten years ago. This row of children nine years ago, this row of children eight years ago . . . With every age the growing human children reached, all the robot children that age were supposed to be destroyed. They were needed only as placeholders and role models. We have human children now who are already twelve years old. Why do these younger robot children still exist? Why weren't the instructions followed?"

Beside Eryn, Ava took a step back into the shadows. But the policewoman grabbed the lead man's arm.

"Please," the policewoman begged, "don't you see?

Those instructions never made sense. They were just . . . wrong. It's wrong to take the life of any sentient being—human *or* robot. Loving parents who had cared for children for a year, two years, *ten* years, *eleven*—how could any loving parent then treat their child like . . . like a piece of trash only worth recycling?"

"It's what we were programmed to do," the lead man said. "It's for the good of society."

"It is *not* for the good of society," the policewoman said. She had switched from begging to sounding more like a judge. "It is a contradiction of everything the new human society should stand for. So . . . parents followed a higher law than their programming. They brought their children here. In secret. To wait until the humans are in charge again. Since we are raising the humans to be good and kind—and not so bound by rigid programming—*they* will allow these children to return. . . ."

Oh, Eryn thought, and she was so surprised she almost laughed. *This woman thinks humans are going to be nicer than robots! She thinks we're going to care more about the robot children than the robots do!*

She thought about how close she had come to swinging the rock column at the baby in the crib. She would have done it if Nick hadn't stopped her.

But then she thought about how she and Nick had run out into a blizzard to try to rescue their parents. How they had agreed that they would never follow the instructions to kill all the robots in the world.

Are humans truly kind after all? she wondered. *Or are we more likely to be cruel? What are we supposed to be like? How are we designed?*

In front of her the man in the suit angrily shook the policewoman's hand off his arm.

"This—this is completely against protocol!" he sputtered. "This is a violation! As an officer of the law, you allowed people to come here to hide their children? Did you just turn a blind eye, or did you actively help them?"

"You're not seeing this the right way," the policewoman said. She was back to pleading again.

"I am seeing this exactly the right way!" the man in the suit shouted. "I see that this egregious violation must be fixed immediately!"

He looked around frantically and picked up a long, thin rock from the ground. Maybe it was the same broken rock column Eryn had used. He swung the rock at the first row of motionless robot children. The policewoman dove in front of him. The rock slammed into the side of her head even as she screamed, "No! Don't do this!"

Maybe it wasn't just the policewoman yelling, "No! Don't do this!" The words were too loud to come from only one voice. Maybe Nick and Lida Mae and Ava and Jackson and some of the robot officials were screaming the same thing. Maybe even Eryn herself was screaming. Everyone around Eryn—even Nick—started running toward the suited man and the policewoman and the rows of children.

But the sound of screaming was too loud to be just from their small crowd of robots and humans. Maybe the cave itself was screaming. The cave seemed to be . . . shifting. Eryn spun her flashlight beam toward the rock wall behind the rows of robot children, and something like double vision hit her eyes. The wall stayed in place, but at the same time a massive creature separated from the wall, stepping out on legs of bulging rocklike muscles, swinging arms and hands that looked capable of crushing anything.

Somehow in all the screaming, Eryn could hear a whisper beside her: Ava gasping, "There were *killer* robots hidden here too?"

FORTY-FIVE

Ava

Ava clutched Lida Mae's arm.

We're the only ones who understand what we're seeing, Ava thought.

Lida Mae whipped her head back toward Ava. Her braids flew wildly.

"My family thought all the killer robots went extinct!" she screamed. "We thought after the humans were gone, the killer robots had no purpose and they just . . . ended! We've never seen any sign of them here. We didn't think they'd be a threat ever again. Honest!"

"I know!" Ava screamed back. That fit with everything she'd learned in the FOR ROBOT ACCESS ONLY room.

But this was absolutely a killer robot emerging from the cave wall. This was absolutely a line of killer robots emerging alongside the first one. They stood nine or ten feet tall, their faces fierce and filled with hate, their bodies muscular under impenetrable-looking armor.

Ava shivered, remembering the ancient scenes of destruction she'd glimpsed in the FOR ROBOT ACCESS ONLY room. She'd seen the battles between humans and robots; she'd seen robots loyal to humans murdered both by humans themselves and by the horrible killer robots they'd created.

Still, she stepped in front of Nick and Eryn, to hide them.

Lida Mae took off running toward the line of killer robots emerging from the wall.

"You already won!" she screamed. "You killed all the humans centuries ago! There's nothing left for you to do!"

Ava resisted the temptation to glare back at Eryn and hiss, *See, that's how to tell a good lie!* She hoped Nick and Eryn had the sense to crouch down, out of sight in the swarm of robots.

But did it matter? Surely the killer robots had sensors to instantly detect the presence of humans. Even Lida Mae's family had a sensor like that, and they didn't have enough technology otherwise to maintain a full robot body.

"Please . . . ," Ava called, feebly.

Oddly, none of the killer robots started advancing

through the crowd, knocking everyone out of the way as they hunted down Nick and Eryn.

Instead, improbably, the killer robot in the center laughed. It was a cold, cruel laugh, but it was a laugh nonetheless.

"We were powerful enough to wipe out the human race," he taunted in a horrible, gravelly voice. "Don't you think we were powerful enough to evolve?"

"We needed a larger purpose," the killer robot beside him agreed, in an even more horrible voice. "Humans proved too easy to kill. Too inconsequential."

"But policing our own species?" the first one added. "Destroying robots who even consider killing their own kind? *That's* a worthy challenge."

Ava suddenly realized that all the regular robot adults had fallen completely silent. They were frozen now, as if too stunned and confused to take any action. There was nothing in their programming for dealing with this situation.

Ava felt exactly the same way.

Then the man in the suit raised his rock column again.

"What you're saying—that's despicable," he said. He lowered the column slightly, as if something new had occurred to him. "Unless . . . could you be reprogrammed again to destroy these robot children? To take care of that for us? According to the proper plan? According to all of our original programming?"

"WE WILL NOT DESTROY THESE ROBOT CHILDREN!" screamed the first killer robot who had emerged from the wall. Now his voice was beyond terrible. It was like hearing a gaping pit speak, like hearing evil itself. "WE USE THEM AS DECOYS! AS A TRAP TO FIND OUT WHO WILL ATTACK OTHER ROBOTS! LIKE YOU! WE FIND THIS OUT . . . SO WE CAN DESTROY ROBOTS LIKE YOU!"

Numbly, Ava remembered the man in the suit smashing the policewoman to the ground. She remembered that he'd wanted to destroy the robot children.

The middle killer robot raised a hand, and a narrow beam of light—a laser, perhaps—shot out.

The man in the suit toppled over.

"That's not the right way to take care of these children!" Lida Mae cried. "To *use* them . . . That's not the right way to live! Didn't you learn anything from the robot-human wars?"

"We learned to gather power for ourselves," the lead killer robot said. "And we learned to wait patiently for the right time to use it."

"And the time is now!" the killer robot beside him screamed.

He reached out—impossibly far—and swiped Lida Mae out of the way, sending her high into the air. Her body arced over all the rows of children and babies she'd been so determined to protect.

And then she landed at the other end of the room with a sick-sounding thud.

She didn't get back up.

Ava almost fell over with fear. She found herself on her knees beside Jackson.

"Jackson!" she hissed at him. "You're still strong, right? Help me get superstrong too, so we can hold off the killer robots and . . ."

And let Eryn and Nick get away, she wanted to say. *Let everyone else escape. Let that EMT find out if Lida Mae and the man in the suit are still alive or dead, and keep them alive, if possible. . . .*

But the lead killer robot strode forward, shoving the adults carelessly aside. He reached out—his arms stretching over half the crowd—and plucked up Ava and Jackson. He let them dangle high above the ground.

"You dare to think you could challenge *us?*" he said. "You dare to think the puny improvements you made to your bodies and minds could last against robots specifically designed to kill?"

"You—you said you'd changed," Ava babbled. "Can't you change . . . more? Why do you have to kill at all?"

"Because we like it!" the killer robot replied. "It's who we are! And look—*this* is how strong your brother is against us!"

Ava saw him rear back, like a baseball pitcher preparing to throw. But it was *Jackson* he had balled up in his hand. It was Jackson he intended to fling against the wall.

Ava reached for her brother, as if she still had hope that she could hold on to him and keep him safe. Her hand brushed skin, and she clutched her fingers together, grabbing desperately. Something came off in her hand: a cord. The cord she and Lida Mae had attached to Jackson's neck to bring him back to consciousness.

As Ava glanced at the cord, the killer robot hurled Jackson's body through the air, toward the solid rock wall.

FORTY-SIX

Jackson

I didn't even get a chance to show how strong I am! Jackson thought, as the wind whistled past his ears. *Nobody knows how much strength it's taken to hold off the all-call from the robot network for so long, when my programming is screaming at me to let go, to tell everything. . . .*

And then he slammed against the wall. The impact was so much harder than he expected that it knocked the air out of his robotic lungs.

It also knocked the resistance out of his mind.

In the instant before he lost consciousness, he let everything he knew transfer to the robot network.

FORTY-SEVEN

Nick

Nick and Eryn ran toward the wall as if they actually thought they could catch Jackson as he slid down the rock. Nick could hear Ava and all the normal robot officials screaming behind him: "No!" "Don't hurt him!" "Please . . ."

And then it was only Ava screaming and pleading, "No, please . . ."

All the normal adult robots went silent. And then, in unison, they let out a pained gasp.

Ava changed what she was screaming.

"Jackson, no!" she cried. "Keep resisting the all-call! Don't let them know anything!"

"I'd say it's too late for that, girly," the killer robot holding Ava taunted. Nick whirled around to see the killer robot shaking Ava back and forth. "Don't you see all those robot faces, how they all looked identically shocked? I'd say everybody in front of me just found out the same information at the same time. . . . Maybe even

I want to find out what it is. Troop, let's link into the fool-robot network."

Nick turned and saw Jackson on the ground, his limbs askew. Maybe he'd broken an arm or a leg. Maybe he'd broken every fake bone in his body.

He didn't move.

"Nick, look," Eryn whispered, putting her hand on Nick's arm and steering him back around to stare at the robots. They had all turned to face Nick and Eryn now, with identical glowers on all their faces.

"Please," Ava cried, still dangling from the giant killer robot's hand. "Don't be angry at my parents! They thought they were doing the right thing, creating Jackson and me . . ."

The killer robot holding Ava didn't even seem to hear her. His expression settled into the same glare as all the regular adult robots.

"Those *human* children are holding instructions to kill every robot in the world?" the killer robot rumbled in his terrible voice. "The human children you were raising to be kind and gentle are already plotting against us? KILL THEM!"

The entire pack of robots began advancing on Nick and Eryn—killer and regular robots together.

FORTY-EIGHT

Eryn

"No!" Eryn yelled. It was a useless word; it was useless to speak at all. She kept screaming anyway. "You don't understand! *We* don't want to kill anybody! Those instructions, those were from before. . . ."

All the robots kept surging toward her and Nick. Were the robot officials coming to protect them? No—the robot officials' faces were almost as menacing as the killer robots'.

When the killer robots linked into the robot network, did they share their way of seeing the world? Eryn wondered. *Have they changed the programming of every robot on the planet?*

"We've got to do something," Nick muttered in her ear. "What can we do?"

Eryn shook her head helplessly.

"You're supposed to take care of us!" Nick yelled at the robots coming toward them. "Not hurt us!"

"Your generation of humans was supposed to be better!" one of the robot officials yelled back. "But you're not! You're just as murderous as your ancestors!"

Something hit Eryn for the first time: No matter how they'd been programmed, all the robots had hoped to survive. Or at least to have their robot children survive. It wasn't just Nick and Eryn's parents and stepparents who'd wanted that and created Ava and Jackson in defiance of the law. It wasn't just the parents who'd hidden their babies and toddlers in this cave instead of letting them be destroyed. It was everyone. Maybe it was because robots were so similar to humans. Maybe they *all* had some humanity at their heart. Or maybe it was because anything alive had the instinct to hold on to life, to treasure it.

The robots were still screaming: "We have to destroy you!" Eryn couldn't even tell if it was killer robots or robot officials saying that.

It's not just Nick and me who are in danger, Eryn thought. *It's every other kid in the world, every embryo waiting to be born. . . .*

If Nick and Eryn didn't figure out how to stop the robots, all of humanity could go extinct again. And this time it would be permanent.

"KILL THEM! KILL THEM!" the giant monster robots at the back chanted, grinning gleefully, as if this was the most fun they'd ever had.

Maybe it didn't even matter how much the killer robots were influencing the others. Maybe any robot would become murderous, hearing about the instructions Nick and Eryn had gotten to kill their own parents, their own teachers—all the robots who had treated them with nothing but kindness their entire lives.

The lead killer robot swung Ava around, as if she were a baton he was using to conduct the "KILL THEM!" chant. She looked terrified and ill, like someone with the worst motion sickness ever, trapped on an amusement park ride. She was shouting something at Nick and Eryn—maybe, "I'm sorry! I'm sorry! I don't want you to die! I didn't mean for this to happen!"

Ava knew we had those instructions to kill robots, and she didn't get mad at us, Eryn thought. *I should have been like Nick and trusted her all along. I'm pretty sure Lida Mae knew about the instructions too. Jackson only knew we had the instructions; he didn't know we were never going to follow them. I wish the robots had done the all-call on Ava's or Lida Mae's brains, not Jackson's. Then they'd understand. . . .*

Eryn saw something whipping around in Ava's hand. A cord. The cord she's grabbed from Jackson's neck.

Is it possible? Eryn wondered. *Is there still a chance?*

A wonderful plan bloomed in Eryn's mind. But everything depended on Ava being able to hear Eryn.

And Ava trusting Eryn enough to follow the plan.

"Ava! Transfer your thoughts and memories into the killer robot's brain!" Eryn screamed. "Do it now! Make them understand everything you understand!"

FORTY-NINE

Ava

Ava saw that Eryn's eyes had locked onto hers, that they followed Ava even as the killer robot whipped Ava's body back and forth through the air. Ava was barely managing not to throw up, but she could tell that Eryn was screaming something at her.

Probably "It's all your fault! Yours and Jackson's! I never wanted stepsiblings anyhow!" Ava thought bitterly.

But Ava had enhanced vision, enhanced hearing. Even as the angry robots closed in on Nick and Eryn, Ava could make out some of Eryn's words, half by lipreading, half by ear: *Transfer . . . now . . . Make . . . understand . . .* She could see Eryn pantomime punching something into Nick's neck.

And then the robots circling around Nick and Eryn blocked Ava's view. She looked instead at the cord dangling from her hand.

Does she mean . . . ? Ava thought. She remembered when she was in the FOR ROBOT ACCESS ONLY room, how she'd thought that she wanted to share her knowledge with other robots and humans. But she hadn't known then that there were still killer robots around; she never would have thought of sharing with them, too. It took a human brain to make that leap.

Does it matter? Ava wondered. *Will this make any difference at all?*

She had to try. For Nick and Eryn's sake. For the sake of humanity.

And for the sake of all robots, too.

As the killer robot swung Ava higher, Ava plunged one end of the cord into his neck. With trembling hands she poked the other end into her own neck.

"Copy!" Ava screamed, her voice shaking. "Copy my brain into his! And into every other robot linked into the network!"

The killer robot swung her down again, and the cord stretched to its very limits.

Will it break before anything happens? Ava wondered. *Do we have enough time?*

Abruptly the killer robot stopped swinging Ava

through the air. The line of monster robots around him stopped chanting. All the angry robots attacking Nick and Eryn stopped completely.

Everyone stood motionless.

And in the silence, across the gulf of the vast cave, Ava's enhanced hearing enabled her to hear Eryn whisper, "Thank you. Thank you, Ava. Thank you, my sister."

EPILOGUE

Everybody

Ava, Eryn, and Nick walked across the newly trimmed grass. It was spring now, and daffodils and crocuses bloomed alongside the well-tended tombstone before them.

The inscription read:

LIDA MAE SPENCER

2004–2016

Lost too soon

Beloved daughter, sister, friend

Ava bent down and tucked another bouquet of flowers into the hollow space between the stone and the dirt. But this bouquet was made of wildflowers: dandelions, violets, clover, and Queen Anne's lace.

"I know these will wilt pretty quickly, but this suits her better than anything we might have bought from a florist,"

Ava said. "At least, that's what *our* Lida Mae told me."

"Yeah," Eryn agreed. "And now that we're here, I see why it would be too creepy for her to look at this."

This tombstone was for the original, *human* Lida Mae, whose spirit and personality had been copied to create the robot Lida Mae.

Nick raised his hand and waved at their Lida Mae, who was standing just outside the gate at the other end of the cemetery. He brought his thumb and forefinger together, making an *okay* sign, and she made the same motion back to him.

The robot official who'd been zapped by the killer robot's death ray had been completely destroyed. But the policewoman had survived being smashed with a rock column, and Lida Mae and Jackson had both survived being thrown across the cave. They'd all needed substantial repairs (and Lida Mae had had the skin on her torso replaced as well). Everyone knew that if they'd been human, all the injured would have been dead. But even Jackson didn't argue that that meant robots were superior to humans.

Because now even Jackson understood that humans had different strengths.

Thanks to Eryn thinking creatively and saving us all,

Nick thought. Then he could practically hear Eryn adding, *With Ava's help.*

Sometimes it was eerie being twins. It was also eerie having parents and stepsiblings who were robots. But the more he got used to it, the more Nick liked it.

It certainly made life interesting.

There were lots of other changes the kids had had to adapt to in the past few months. The entire family (steps and all) had relocated to Kentucky, just outside the Mammoth Cave nature preserve. Ava and Jackson's parents, Brenda and Michael, had taken jobs bringing the babies and children from the cave back to life, and updating them after their years in storage. They were even retrofitting the young robots, making it so they could grow and change just like Ava and Jackson.

That, amazingly, was entirely legal now.

Nick and Eryn's mom, Denise, counseled the restored kids and their families about how to handle their new chance at life.

And Nick and Eryn's dad, Donald, was busy building hotels for those families to stay in as they came to pick up their kids. He'd also built houses for Lida Mae's family to live in outside the cave, now that all of them were fully repaired and restored. It was a good thing Jackson had made himself so strong and fast, because Donald needed all the help he could get.

Sometimes Donald talked about getting Michael or Brenda to give him the same kind of superhuman powers. But then he'd always reconsider: "I think changes like that are better for the younger generation. I've spent too many years with a weak and slow body—I'm not sure I could handle all that power."

Sometimes Eryn wondered if he was just being kind to his kids, trying not to thrust too much change at them at once.

Little did he know . . .

"You in?" Ava asked.

Eryn and Nick both nodded.

"And Jackson said I could vote on his behalf—he's in too," Nick said.

"And I have Lida Mae's vote," Eryn said. "It's yes."

"Okay, then," Ava said. She tried to pretend that her hands weren't shaking. But why should they shake? She wasn't in this alone. "It's official. The five of us will go out and hunt down all the other killer robots still hidden in the world and . . ." She pulled an innocent-looking cord from her jeans pocket. "And teach them a better way of viewing the world. One that won't destroy *anyone.*"

Ava knew that there was still the small matter of convincing their parents and stepparents that the five kids were the right ones for that particular task. But she knew they were up to it.

Hadn't they already proved they could save the world?

"Hey, wait for us!" she heard off in the distance.

She turned and saw Jackson coming toward the cemetery. He was riding on the shoulder of one of the killer robots—actually, a *former* killer robot. Originally, none of the killer robots had had names, because they'd been practically interchangeable. But they'd all begun choosing what they wanted to be called.

This one insisted his name was Ralph.

The ground shook a little as he stomped forward on his boulderlike legs, but he grinned and waved his arm at all the kids just as joyfully as Jackson did.

"Have you voted already?" Jackson called as he and Ralph approached the cemetery gate where Lida Mae was standing. "Ralph says he wants to come too."

"Is that all right?" Ralph asked hesitantly, his timid voice sounding almost comical coming from his massive head.

Eryn started trying to telegraph a message to Nick

with her eyes: *Are we ready for this? Working as a team not just with robots, but former* killer *robots too?*

But then she gave up. She knew what his answer would be. Yes.

That was her answer too.

Before either of them could reply, Lida Mae spoke for all of them from beside the gate.

"Of course!" she said. "The more the merrier!"

Ralph responded by reaching out—impossibly far— and scooping her up and putting her on his other shoulder.

"I just thought it'd be good to have *two* robots on our team with superhuman strength," Jackson explained.

"Along with two robots who don't need superhuman strength to be amazing," Ava retorted.

"And two humans," Eryn said softly. "Two humans who are glad to still be around. And . . . who know it's best for both robots and humans if we all work together."

"We all know that now," Jackson called to her from across the cemetery. His enhanced hearing had picked up even her near whisper.

Eryn looked down at the tombstone one last time. It wasn't just the original Lida Mae she wanted to remember. It was two scientists who had probably died without ever being buried, but who had held on to hope long enough to make sure the human race could start again. It was a small group of desperate robots who, in a time of cataclysmic war, had chosen a path nobody else saw.

"We're doing this for you," Eryn whispered.

Nick slugged her shoulder.

"Who are you kidding?" he asked. "We're doing this for ourselves! Because it will be fun!"

Ava stepped between them and put her arms around both of her stepsiblings.

"We're doing this for everyone," she said firmly. "For humans and robots and enhanced robots and former killer robots . . . We're doing this for everyone's future. Because now? Now we *all* have one."

A READING GROUP GUIDE FOR
Under Their Skin, Book Two:
In Over Their Heads
By Margaret Peterson Haddix

About the Book

Nick and Eryn must figure out a way to save the world without sacrificing their newly discovered family in this follow-up to *Under Their Skin*.

In *Under Their Skin*, twins Nick and Eryn successfully met their new stepsiblings, Ava and Jackson. But in doing so, the twins found themselves on a mission to discover how to prevent humanity from facing certain doom.

Now their two families are joined together to save not only themselves, but everyone—human *and* robotic. Can they figure out how before it's too late?

Discussion Questions

1. How is Ava different from her brother? Find quotes from the novel to support your opinion.

2. Eryn is aware that "the papers under Nick's shirt said that even the caretaker robots were dangerous and had to be destroyed. Even the robots like Eryn's parents. And Ava and Jackson." What should Eryn do? If you had to "destroy" your family and those you love to save your world, would you do it?

3. Nick recognizes that "he was carrying instructions that said his life, his sister's life—no, the very survival of humanity—depended on him and Eryn becoming murderers . . ." After reading this quote, do you believe that Nick sees destroying robots as heroic or savage? What evidence in the rest of novel supports your view?

4. Do you think that Eryn and Nick ever truly believe that they will kill their family? Explain your response.

5. Where is the novel set? When do you think the story takes place? What evidence do you have that supports your conjectures?

6. In the first half of the novel, all four siblings know what the papers say, but for the most part, they keep their feelings to themselves. What are their differing thoughts about the papers' instructions? What do their different reactions to the papers tell us about the characters' personalities? Which character's attitude corresponds most closely with yours?

7. "Ava did not envy Nick and Eryn, having their every move psychoanalyzed and explained to them their entire lives." Find places in the novel where Denise, the human twins' mom, explains her kids' lives to them. Would you prefer a parent who understands preteen psychology or one who does not?

8. In the first book, Eryn and Nick are angry that they have been lied to, or at least not told the truth. In this second book, we see that all of the kids, including Jackson and Ava, are worried about telling the truth and are suspicious of others. Why does this distrust happen?

9. "It felt like the surprise and fear mingled in their expressions were her fault." What does this quote tell us about Lida Mae?

10. How do the different characters react to Jackson's "breakdowns"? How are these reactions similar to the different ways that some people react to people who have mental breakdowns?

11. How does the human and robot conflict in the story relate to conflicts in today's world? Is the conflict between the humans and robots caused by prejudice and fear? Explain why or why not. Do you believe that the robots and humans in the story could live together in peace?

12. Reread chapter 12. Jackson is hiding under a blanket in the back of the van. What is Jackson thinking and feeling before Dad comes back from the store?

13. Can one kill a machine? If you kill a robot, as Eryn almost does, is that murder?

14. Is Lida Mae an adult in a child's body? What evidence from the novel supports your opinion?

15. What is the purpose of the prologue? What questions do

you have after reading it? How does the prologue make you feel? Are your questions answered by the end of the book?

16. Before Ava announces the fact, did you uncover Lida Mae's secret? Did the author provide any evidence earlier in the novel to allude to Lida Mae's secret?

17. If the chapters were not labeled with the character's name, could you tell if the chapter was from Ava's, Jackson's, Eryn's or Nick's perspective? Why or why not?

18. In what ways are Jackson and Ava more like humans than robots?

19. Using evidence from this series, who is more durable: a robot or a human? Explain your answer.

20. Explain what has happened to Lida Mae's family.

21. How are the killer robots defeated? What is the message or theme that the defeat demonstrates?

22. Eryn says to herself, "This woman thinks humans are going to be nicer than robots!" What do you think? Which group is nicer: humans or robots?

23. What do you think is the purpose of the epilogue?

Guide written by Shari Conradson, an English, drama, and history teacher at Brook Haven School in California.

This guide has been provided by Simon & Schuster for classroom, library, and reading group use. It may be reproduced in its entirety or excerpted for these purposes.